Levi gripped her ar ... **tipped her chin up** "—it's just paint."

She shook her head. "It's more than that," she said. "It's a message that they aren't done with me. I killed one of theirs."

"So did I," he said.

She looked up at him. "Then you'll probably be next. Neither one of us will be safe until we stop them."

He forced a smile. "Then it's a good thing we've got each other's backs." He pulled her into his arms and hugged her.

Slowly, her arms found their way around him, and she leaned her cheek against his chest.

"Go ahead," he said. "Lean on me."

She absorbed his heat for a few minutes more.

And then he leaned back, tipping her head up again and forcing her to stare into his eyes. "You know what you need to do, don't you?"

"Yes. No." She frowned. "Maybe? Where are you going with this?"

He chuckled. "We've got to crack this case wide open."

This book is dedicated to my sister, Delilah Devlin, who has first look at my work, helps me brainstorm when I'm stuck and keeps me straight.

To my niece, Kelly, for transcribing my dictation overnight. I couldn't do this without you.

For my mother, who loved to read and could never be found without a book in her hand. I miss you, Mom.

SETUP AT WHISKEY GULCH

—

New York Times Bestselling Author
ELLE JAMES

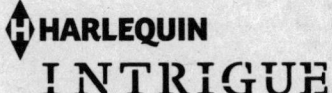

HARLEQUIN
INTRIGUE

HARLEQUIN®
INTRIGUE™

ISBN-13: 978-1-335-55571-7

Setup at Whiskey Gulch

Copyright © 2022 by Mary Jernigan

This edition published by arrangement with Harlequin Books S.A.

For questions and comments about the quality of this book, please contact us at CustomerService@Harlequin.com.

Harlequin Enterprises ULC
22 Adelaide St. West, 41st Floor
Toronto, Ontario M5H 4E3, Canada
www.Harlequin.com

Printed in U.S.A.

Elle James, a *New York Times* bestselling author, started writing when her sister challenged her to write a romance novel. She has managed a full-time job and raised three wonderful children, and she and her husband even tried ranching exotic birds (ostriches, emus and rheas). Ask her, and she'll tell you what it's like to go toe-to-toe with an angry 350-pound bird! Elle loves to hear from fans at ellejames@earthlink.net or ellejames.com.

Visit the Author Profile page at Harlequin.com.

CAST OF CHARACTERS

Levi Warren—Former Delta Force soldier who left active duty to save his marriage only to end in divorce. Takes job with the Outriders for a chance to start over.

Dallas Jones—Former US Army Military Police, working as a deputy sheriff in Whiskey Gulch.

Trace Travis—Former Delta Force who shares his inheritance with his father's bastard son and builds a security agency employing former military.

Irish Monahan—Former Delta Force soldier who left active duty to make a life out of the line of fire. Working for Trace Travis as a member of the Outriders.

Matt Hennessey—Prior service, marine and town bad boy, now half owner of the Whiskey Gulch Ranch and the Outriders Agency.

Harold Sims—Turning his life around after rehab.

Johnny Marks—One of the leaders of the Snakes Motorcycle gang.

Jimmy Marks—One of the leaders of the Snakes Motorcycle gang.

Raymond Sweeney—Owner of and bartender at Sweeney's Bar.

Evan Billings—Part-time janitor at the dance hall.

Sean Langley—Mechanic at the tire store.

Chapter One

Deputy Dallas Jones left the diner on Main Street with a full cup of coffee, ready to go to work. She liked the graveyard shift on weeknights, which were usually pretty quiet and required her to drink coffee to stay awake.

Things were different in Whiskey Gulch on Friday and Saturday. With townspeople and ranch hands wanting to spend their paychecks at the local bars, she didn't need the pick-me-up.

She'd just set her cup in the cup holder of her service SUV when Ouida Sims hurried up to her window.

"Deputy Jones," she called out. "I'm so glad I caught you."

Dallas started to climb out of her vehicle.

Ouida shook her head. "You don't have to get out. I just wanted to ask you to keep an eye out for Harold tonight. I haven't seen him since lunch, and I'm getting worried. He's not answering his cell phone, which isn't terribly unusual since reception can be kind of spotty out here. But it's getting late."

"What were his plans for the afternoon?" Dallas asked.

The fifty-something-year-old woman with graying blond hair wrung her hands. "He's been farm sitting for the Thatchers out at the Rafter T Ranch while they're on vacation in Mexico. He might just have gotten busy and lost track of time, but I'd sure feel a lot better if I knew for sure."

Dallas nodded. "I'll head out there and see what I can find out."

Ouida smiled. "Thank you. I appreciate it. He's been trying so hard to get himself back on track since coming back from rehab. I love that man. I'd hate to see him slip back off that wagon, not that I think he would. He promised me he'd stay clean, and I believe him." She gave Dallas a crooked smile. "But I worry."

"I understand," Dallas said. "I'll look for him."

Ouida stepped back from the SUV and waved as Dallas pulled out of the parking lot.

In the few months Dallas had worked in the small Texas town of Whiskey Gulch, she'd gotten to know a lot of the locals, including Ouida and Harold Sims.

Ouida worked as a waitress at the diner, and

Harold took on any job he could get since he'd left rehab for alcohol addiction.

Harold had been out of rehab now for over a month and seemed to be doing well. He always had a smile for Dallas when she drove by in her old pickup truck or her service SUV. Dallas didn't mind checking up on him, and it gave her a purpose for at least a small portion of the evening that she'd be on shift.

For the most part, she liked working in Whiskey Gulch. It had taken her a few months to get used to the slower pace after leaving the military. She thought she wouldn't have much in common with the locals, many of whom had never served in the armed forces, but then she'd met Trace Travis and his half brother Matt Hennessey.

Both men had served in Special Operations Forces. Trace had been Delta Force. Matt spent time in Marine Force Reconnaissance. They were highly skilled in warfare and tactics. Since his return to his home at Whiskey Gulch Ranch, Trace Travis had hired more of his military buddies to work the ranch and to set up an agency to help others in need. Which had proved handy when things had gotten a little out of hand and dangerous in Whiskey Gulch a couple of months back.

While it was a slower pace most of the time,

they'd had their share of major crime in Whiskey Gulch. Still, Dallas liked it there. The number of incidents were far fewer than what she might have found in places like Houston, Austin or San Antonio. There was just enough going on to keep her interest.

Dallas headed south out of Whiskey Gulch toward the Rafter T Ranch, always conscious of her speed, knowing she set the example for the young folk. She lifted her coffee mug and sipped, placing it back in the cup holder as she neared a curve in the road. She glanced down for only a second, and when she looked up again, a man staggered into the road in front of her. She slammed on her brakes and turned her wheel sharply, skidding sideways in an attempt to avoid hitting him, but he was too close. Because she had been slowing through the curve, she wasn't going fast when the metal of her passenger side door connected with the man. Still, she bumped him enough to send him flying backward.

Dallas slid off the edge of the road into the ditch. When she finally got control of her steering wheel, she drove out of the ditch onto the road, her hands shaking, her pulse racing through her veins. She switched on her lights to warn any other vehicles that might happen upon them. She parked her car on the shoulder of the road, jumped out and ran back to where the man lay in the gravel. As she ran, she clicked the button on her radio and spoke into the mic. "This is Deputy Dallas Jones. I need an ambulance out on Old Mill Highway, three miles south of Whiskey Gulch. Send the sheriff as well. I have a middle-aged man on the ground who was hit by a vehicle." *My vehicle.*

"Shoot, shoot, shoot," Dallas muttered as she dropped to her knees beside the man. "Hey, mister, talk to me. Please, talk to me."

He lay facedown in the gravel, completely still.

Hesitant to move him to avoid causing more injury, she reached around him, touching her fingers to the base of his throat to check for a pulse. When she felt none, she had to roll him over on his back so she could perform CPR. She carefully turned him over and again felt for a pulse. "Sir, can you hear me?"

No response and still no pulse. She started CPR, alternating between thirty compressions and two breaths, pausing every so often to search for a pulse. Her headlights were her only source of light, and her body cast a shadow over the man's face. She worked over him until the ambulance arrived, sirens screaming. Her arms ached by the time an EMT took over. Another EMT brought out a defibrillator, ripped open the man's shirt and laid the paddles on his chest. When they shocked him, his body jerked, elevated and immediately plopped back to the ground.

After three shocks, the EMT shook his head. "He's gone."

Dallas stood back, her heart still racing, her eyes burning.

One of the EMTs shone a flashlight in the man's face. It was bloody and bruised, but he looked familiar. Dallas recognized him, and her heart sank. The man was the one she had been looking for, Harold Sims. Not only had she run over the man, now she had the dreadful task of telling Ouida Sims her husband was dead.

LEVI HAD SPENT the evening parked on the bluffs south of town, staring at billions of stars in the Texas sky. That was, until the clouds rolled in, obstructing his view. The only time he could remember seeing that many stars had been when he'd been on watch in Afghanistan one cold winter night. Like then, he was thinking back over his life and wondering what his wife was up to.

Ex-wife.

In Afghanistan, he'd had a video call with her prior to the mission under the stars. She'd seemed distracted when he'd called, as if she didn't have the time or desire to talk to him. That feeling had eaten into his concentration throughout the mission. So much so, he'd decided to get out of the military and the Delta Force team he considered family, in an attempt to save his marriage. He'd been on deployment in Afghanistan when his enlistment was up. He'd decided then that he would separate from the army as soon as he got back.

A lot of good that had done. He'd come home to an empty apartment and divorce papers to sign. He'd given up the military for no reason. Yeah, he probably could have gone back on active duty. His special ops training would have gotten him right back on board with his old team, probably, but with a wrecked marriage under his belt, he wasn't so sure he wanted to go back.

The life of a Delta Force operative was consumed by training and missions. There wasn't much time for anything else. No, he wanted to give it a chance, and see what life on the outside was like. Maybe he wasn't cut out for it. In that case, he would reenlist. But by then, the army might not want him back. Still, it was a risk he was willing to take.

He'd lain under the stars on the bluff just south of Whiskey Gulch for a couple of hours, trying to figure out if he'd made the right decision by taking a job with Trace Travis, a former Delta Force operative just like him. Could he use his training to help others in the civilian world?

Only time would tell.

Now that he'd committed to the plan, he needed to stick with it long enough to determine if this was the right path for him. As it neared midnight, clouds drifted in. Levi realized he needed to get back to Whiskey Gulch Ranch. He'd have to get up early the next day to do chores. When they weren't solving cases for other people, the men of the Outriders organization kept busy ranching, which also kept them from having idle hands, which could be troublesome for an adrenaline junkie, like many of the Deltas were.

Levi climbed into his pickup and headed back to Whiskey Gulch. On the way, he noticed flashing lights. He slowed as he approached an ambulance and a deputy sheriff's SUV blocking the roadway. He pulled over. He recognized the deputy as Dallas Jones, the only female on the force.

From what Trace had told him, Deputy Jones was prior military as well, having served as an army MP, military police. It made sense she chose law enforcement to put her skills to good use. He wondered why she had gotten off active duty. Had she been medically discharged, or had she left on her own terms?

Levi had met Deputy Jones shortly after he'd gone to work for Trace Travis and the Outriders. He hadn't really thought much about her other than that she seemed nice-looking for a female cop and she was somewhat reserved. But now, standing in the headlights from her service vehicle and the flashing lights of the ambulance, she seemed pale, with her brow knit in a fierce frown. Unable to get past the ambulance and the SUV, and curious about what had happened, Levi parked his truck and got down.

He approached Deputy Jones. "Anything I can do to help?"

She shook her head slowly as if in a daze. "He came out of nowhere and stepped in front of my vehicle."

The anguish in her tone hit Levi square in the gut. "What happened?"

Deputy Jones swallowed hard. "His wife…" Her eyes rounded. "Oh, dear Lord, I have to tell his wife." She looked around as if ready to bolt.

Levi gripped Deputy Jones's arms. "Hey, you're not going anywhere right now. Why don't you just tell me what happened?"

She shook her head. "I can't."

"At least tell me who it is?" Levi stared down into her eyes, willing her to look into his.

"It's Harold," she said, "Harold Sims. His wife was worried about him. She asked me to go check up on him." The deputy stared up at Levi's eyes. "I was on my way out to the Rafter T Ranch to see if I could find him. His wife said that he was supposed to have been home earlier."

"Where's the Rafter T Ranch?" Levi asked.

The deputy tilted her head toward the south. "Another couple of miles. I wasn't expecting to see him this soon, not out in the middle of nowhere on the side of the road." She swallowed hard, her eyes welling with unshed tears. "He stepped out in front of my vehicle. I couldn't stop. I slammed on my brakes, but it was too late." She hung her head. "I did CPR… I did everything I could…" When she looked up again, the anguish in her gaze made Levi's chest tighten.

He hated seeing her so distraught. He tipped her chin up, forcing her to stare into his eyes. "It's not your fault," he said in a gentle tone.

She gazed at him as if seeing far beyond where he stood. "I should have been able to do something. Those men shouldn't be dead because of me," she said.

Levi frowned. "Was there more than one man?"

The deputy blinked, and a single tear slipped

from the corner of her eye. "Sorry, no, there was only one. Harold." She backed away and shoved a hand through her hair. "That was another..." She shook her head. "Never mind."

Levi frowned. He could have sworn she was about to say that was another time. He wondered what other time that could have been that left her face so haunted. The tall and fully capable deputy seemed extremely vulnerable at that moment.

Though he was tired and ready for bed, Levi couldn't leave her standing there alone. He touched her shoulder. "Mind if I wait with you?"

Deputy Jones blinked and looked around as if trying to decipher her whereabouts before finally coming to her senses. She straightened her shoulders. "There's no need to wait. I'll move my car."

"No hurry," he said.

She strode to her vehicle, climbed in and moved it onto the shoulder. Then she got out a couple of flares, lit them and placed them several yards to the front and rear of the accident scene. So far, no other vehicles had come along the road. She stood, ready to direct traffic around the ambulance if anyone came along.

Levi stood by throughout.

She frowned when she spotted him again and

walked over to where he stood on the side of the road. "You really should move along."

"And I will," he said. "When I know you're okay."

She lifted her chin. "I'm fine. The sheriff is on his way out, along with a tow truck. I'm sure that they're going to want to tow my vehicle in as they investigate the case."

"If they are going to tow your vehicle, you'll need a ride home. I'd be glad to give you a lift."

She shook her head. "I can catch a ride back to the station with the sheriff."

Levi nodded. It made sense. "Okay, but I'll wait until the sheriff gets here, and then I'll leave."

She shrugged. "Suit yourself. Just stay out of the way of the first responders doing their jobs."

Lights flashed in the distance coming from the south, and they weren't the kind of lights that indicated a four-wheeled vehicle. Instead, they were individual headlights.

As they neared, Levi could hear the roar of the engines. The headlights were almost on them before Levi could distinguish the shape of motorcycles with men riding them.

They slowed as they approached the ambulance, lights still flashing. The man in the lead rolled to a stop next to Deputy Jones. "What's happening?"

The deputy was all business now. She stared across at the leader of the motorcycle group. "There's been an accident. Please, move along."

The man had long silver hair pulled back into a ponytail at the back of his head and sported a salt-and-pepper gray mustache. He wore a sleeveless tank top with a leather vest over it. He'd rolled past Levi to stop in front of Deputy Jones.

Levi caught a glimpse of the back of his vest, where a white tightly coiled snake contrasted sharply with the dark leather. The other members of his gang wore leather vests or leather jackets with the same coiled snake emblazoned on the back. One of the men climbed off his motorcycle and walked over to where the ambulance stood.

"Sir," Deputy Jones called out, "please stay back."

He ignored her and kept walking.

The deputy turned to the man who appeared to be the leader of the motorcycle gang. "Please, tell your men to stay back."

For a long moment the man stared down at her. Finally, he revved his engine and yelled at the man who was closing in on the ambulance. "Hey, Bulldog," he called out.

The man turned around.

The leader jerked his head toward his bike.

The man called out to him. "Looks like Sims."

Stiffening, the leader frowned. "Are you sure?"

His gang member nodded as he returned to his bike. "It's Sims all right."

The lips of the man with the silver hair tightened into a thin line. "Let's go."

The men revved their motorcycle engines to a deafening roar. They moved past Levi and the deputy, then hit their throttles and blasted away.

Levi could see the tension leave Deputy Jones's shoulders upon their departure.

No sooner had their taillights disappeared than another set of headlights came from the direction of Whiskey Gulch, along with the rotating red and blue lights of another sheriff's vehicle and the amber lights atop a tow truck.

Again, the deputy tensed. The sheriff's vehicle pulled up behind hers and parked. Sheriff Thomas Greer climbed out and closed the distance between himself and the deputy. "Hey, Dallas," he said. "Got word you needed some help out here. Whatcha got?"

The deputy nodded. "Yes, sir." She turned and fell in step with him, moving toward the gurney the EMTs were loading into the ambulance.

Levi stood back, not wanting to interfere with the sheriff's business.

When they arrived beside the gurney, the EMT stepped aside and let the sheriff pull the sheet away from the victim's face.

Sheriff Greer shook his head. "Harold Sims all right," he said. "I really thought he was on the wagon for good this time."

The sheriff's mouth was pressed into a thin line as he listened to Deputy Jones explain what had happened.

When she finished, he said, "You know I have to put you on administrative leave until the investigation is complete."

"Sir," she said, "you're already shorthanded."

The sheriff nodded. "I know."

"I want to be involved in the investigation," the deputy insisted.

The sheriff shook his head. "Can't let you, since you were the one to hit him."

"But you heard me—it wasn't intentional. He stepped out in front of me."

The sheriff shrugged. "It doesn't matter. It's county policy. If a law enforcement officer is involved in a fatal accident, they have to be placed on administrative leave until the investigation is complete and the officer is cleared of any wrongdoing."

"I understand." Her shoulders sagged. "What about the rest of my shift?" she asked.

"I'll fill in until I can get somebody else on duty."

"But you just put in a full day's work," she said.

"I'll be all right," he said. "Let me give you a ride back to the station."

"Sir." Levi stepped forward. "If you need to stay and investigate the scene, I can take the deputy back to Whiskey Gulch."

The sheriff's eyes narrowed as he stared across at Levi. "Are you one of the new guys Trace Travis has working out at Whiskey Gulch Ranch?"

"Yes, sir." Levi nodded and stuck his hand out. "I'm Levi Warren."

"Are you also former military?"

Levi nodded again. "Yes, sir."

"What branch?"

Levi squared his shoulders, standing tall and proud. "Army. Delta Force."

The sheriff gave him a slight smile. "Thank you for your service."

"Thank you for yours, Sheriff."

The sheriff turned to his deputy. "Do you want to ride with Mr. Warren?"

"I'd rather stay and help you investigate the scene," Dallas said.

The sheriff shook his head. "I'm sorry, Dallas. Other than taking your statement, I can't have you help me. You should head back to town if you don't mind riding with Levi. I'll need your written statement about what happened."

The deputy nodded. "I'll get right on it." She turned to Levi. "If you can get me back to the sheriff's station, I'd appreciate it."

The deputy and Levi were climbing into Levi's truck when the tow truck arrived. As Levi drove past the scene, the deputy's gaze locked on the ambulance and the sheriff, her head swiveling.

"Hey, look," Levi said, "I'm sorry about what happened."

The deputy sat and stared straight forward through the windshield. "What do you have to be sorry about? You weren't the one who hit him."

"You can't blame yourself. It wasn't your fault," he said.

She turned toward him. "Then whose was it? I need to be involved in the investigation. I need to know why he staggered out in front of me with his head bleeding."

Levi frowned. "His head was bleeding?"

The deputy's forehead dented as if she were concentrating. "Yes, his forehead was already bleeding when he stepped out onto the highway."

"You need to make sure that goes into your written statement."

She nodded, her forehead creasing even deeper. "I'll want to see the medical examiner's report as well, but dammit—" she slammed her fist into her palm "—they probably won't let me since I'm off the investigation."

"Surely the sheriff will share information with you if you ask him."

She nodded. "Most likely he will. The sheriff's a good guy. Question is, why was Harold Sims's forehead bleeding prior to impact? Had he fallen or had somebody hurt him?"

"Hopefully the medical examiner can shed some light on that." Levi glanced across the console at Dallas. She sat staring forward, her brow deeply dented. "Are you all right?"

She frowned. "I'm fine, but Harold isn't. I have to know if someone is responsible for him being out here, alone. There has to be a reason he stumbled out onto the highway."

Silence stretched between them.

Levi wanted to distract her to give her a reprieve from the trauma. "Travis told me something about how you were an MP in the army…?" Levi said.

The deputy glanced away and nodded. "I was."

"How many years did you have on active duty?" he asked.

"Eight," she said.

"That's a lot of years to walk away from," he said.

She nodded. "It was time."

"I take it you left under your own steam?"

Again, she nodded. She shot a look in his direction. "What about you?"

He shrugged. "It was time," he said, echoing her words.

"How many years?" she persisted.

"Eleven."

Her lips quirked on the ends. "That's a lot of years to walk away from. You were on the downhill slide to retirement."

His lips twisted. "I got out to save my marriage."

"Nice," she said. "At least she appreciated it. At least you have a marriage to save."

He shook his head. "Didn't quite work out that way."

She shot a look toward him, but by that time they were pulling up to the sheriff's station in Whiskey Gulch.

"Do you want me to wait for you while you write your statement?" he asked.

She shook her head. "No, I have my truck here."

"Would you like to get a beer or a cup of coffee afterward?"

She frowned across at him. "You're persistent, aren't you?"

He shrugged. "I have nothing better to do at this hour."

She snorted softly. "Most people would sleep at this time."

He nodded. "And I usually do, except tonight would have been my ten-year anniversary. Didn't feel much like sleeping."

"You could have been hanging out with your buddies at Whiskey Gulch Ranch," she pointed out.

He nodded. "I could have, but I didn't feel like it."

She glanced toward the station, and then back to him. "Well, it will take me a minimum of twenty minutes."

He shifted into Park. "I'll be here. I could use the company."

She gave him a wry grin. "I guess I could, too."

While she was inside writing up her statement, he sat in his truck wondering why he was extending his time with the deputy.

He had gone out driving by himself, wanting to get away from people. After staring up at the stars for a couple of hours, he'd only felt even more intensely lonely. Sharing her company over a cup of coffee or a beer would help pass the time until morning and another day where he would help on the ranch until his next assignment, or rather his first assignment with the Outriders. He didn't mind helping with the ranch chores. The hard physical labor helped him work out some of the demons still eating at him over the loss of his marriage. It wasn't like he was trying to hit on the deputy. He just really didn't want to be alone on what would have been his anniversary.

He'd known his marriage was on the rocks, but he hadn't understood just how much on the rocks it had been until his wife had hit him with the divorce papers when he'd gotten home from deployment. He'd committed to getting out of the military, hoping that it would make CeCe realize how much he wanted to save their marriage. By the time he returned to the States, it'd been eight months since he'd seen her. He had refused to discuss separation until he got back. When he walked into their house, though, he'd known it was over.

Her stuff had been gone, along with most of his. The only thing she hadn't moved out was his gun safe and the old recliner he'd brought into the marriage and refused to let go of, even when she'd redecorated the entire house. She'd refused to take his phone calls. When he'd gone by her office and followed her to her new home, he'd found that she was living with another man. His marriage was truly over.

That was when he'd signed the divorce papers. Thankfully, that was the same day he'd received a call from his friend Trace Travis. Levi had needed an excuse to leave the empty shell of his home and start over.

The problem was, he wasn't sure if he was heartbroken over the demise of his marriage or if he was more upset over having failed. Levi had been good at just about everything he'd done in his life. From Little League baseball to being the quarterback on his high school football team. Everything he'd done he'd succeeded at, including marrying the head cheerleader, his high school sweetheart.

CeCe hadn't been particularly thrilled when he'd joined the army, but she'd hung in with him, liking the fact that he had gone on to be accepted into Delta Force, an elite force of the army. But she hadn't quite realized how much time he would be spending away from her. He suspected like many of the other army wives of the Delta Force, she'd gotten lonely and found someone else who would be there more often than he was.

Levi had done a little bit of investigating to

find out her new lover had nothing to do with the military. He was an insurance salesman.

Before he realized it, Deputy Jones was coming out of the station. No longer wearing her uniform, she wore faded blue jeans and an equally faded blue chambray shirt. Her sandy-blond hair hung down below her shoulders, free of the ponytail she'd worn earlier. She stopped beside his window, her gray eyes meeting his.

Levi lowered the glass.

The deputy cocked an eyebrow. "Meet you at Sweeney's Bar?"

He nodded.

Jones climbed into what looked like a 1960s model Ford pickup truck. It took several times cranking the starter before the engine engaged with a coughing sputter and then a roar. The deputy shifted into Reverse, backed out of the parking space in front of the sheriff's office and drove out onto Main Street.

Levi's pulse quickened as he followed Dallas the couple of blocks to the closest of the two bars. He should have left after dropping her off. But something about this woman made him want to be with her. If only for a few minutes more.

Chapter Two

Five vehicles sat in the bar parking lot when Dallas pulled in. She was glad she'd taken the time to change. The last thing she needed was to show up at the bar in uniform.

Not all the cowboys in the county appreciated law enforcement, especially at Sweeney's Bar. She'd busted up several fights and had arrested more than one of Sweeney's customers over the past few months.

She parked her old truck by backing it into a parking space. She never knew when it wouldn't start, and it was always good to have it pointed outward in case somebody had to jump-start her battery or she simply needed a quick getaway.

Levi backed in beside her in his newer-model sleek black truck, a sharp contrast to hers, which was over fifty years old. Her vehicle had its issues, and it didn't have air-conditioning, but she couldn't part with it. She'd sold her Jeep and now strictly relied on the red-and-white 1967 Ford pickup.

She didn't want to admit it out loud, but she suspected that she was paying a form of penance by suffering the Texas heat without the air-conditioning. And every time she had to work on the engine, the pain of banging her knuckles against metal reminded her that she was still alive.

The former owner of the pickup was dead.

Dallas shifted into Park as guilt washed over her. What was she doing at a bar having a drink with another man?

It's not like it's a date.

Not that it would have mattered if it was. Her fiancé had been dead for two years. How long was long enough to mourn the man you'd loved? She could have gone home and gone to bed, but every time she closed her eyes, she either saw Harold stepping out in front of her SUV or Brian lying in the Afghan dirt, his body bloody and shredded by the IED that had exploded under his truck.

Her fingers gripped the steering wheel until her knuckles turned white, and her heart raced with the same panic attacks she still suffered two years after Brian's death. Dallas had been in charge of making certain that convoy arrived safely to the forward operating base. Six soldiers had died in that explosion set off by a remote detonator.

Dallas and several others had done everything they could, using self-aid buddy care, but their efforts hadn't been enough when the wounds had been so grievous. The men had bled out in minutes. She'd watched the life fade from Brian's eyes. His last word was him calling out her name, "Dallas."

A tap on her window brought her back to the present.

Levi opened her truck door. "Are you okay?"

Not really, but she wouldn't admit it out loud. What kind of law enforcement officer fell apart at an accident scene or sitting in her truck? "I'm fine," she said. "But I could use a beer."

Levi cupped her elbow and guided her into Sweeney's Bar & Grill.

Sweeney's place was one of two bars in Whiskey Gulch. Situated on the north edge of Whiskey Gulch, it was the favorite of the cowboys and ranchers coming in from a hard day's work.

The other bar was more of a dance hall that catered to the rowdier crowds. If a person just wanted a beer or maybe a sandwich, Sweeney's was the place to go during the week, and it usually shut down around one thirty in the morning.

The owner, Ray Sweeney, had inherited the

bar from his father and hadn't put a dime into the upkeep. He didn't pay his staff much, expecting them to make it up in tips. Business was usually good because of the location. His bar was the closest to town and easiest to get to and from.

"Do you want to sit at a table or the bar?" Levi asked.

Sitting at a table with a former Delta seemed a little too intimate for Dallas. "The bar will be fine." She crossed the floor and slid onto a bar stool. Levi straddled the one to her right.

A waitress walked up to the bar and plunked her tray on the countertop. "Howdy, y'all," she said. "I'm Angie. I can get you a beer. If you want anything fancy, you'll have to wait for the bartender." She yelled across the room at one of the other waitresses. "Hey, Lucy, where'd Bernie go?"

"He had to leave. His wife was sick," Lucy said over her shoulder as she set bottles of beer in front of three men dressed in jeans and dirt-streaked shirts. Their faces were tanned a ruddy brown as if they'd been baked in the sun.

"Is Ray back?" Angie asked.

At that moment, Ray Sweeney pushed through the swinging door from the kitchen and strode into the barroom. The man wore a clean white T-shirt, and his salt-and-pepper gray hair was damp and slicked back from his forehead. "What do ya need?" he asked.

"I need two whiskeys on the rocks and a couple of Bud Lights in the bottle."

The waitress turned to Dallas and Levi. "Sweeney'll take care of you."

Sweeney filled the waitress's order, then turned to Levi and Dallas. "What can I get you two?"

"I'll have a draft beer," Dallas said.

"Make that two," Levi added.

Sweeney filled two mugs, one at a time, from the tap and set them in front of the two, and then leaned on the counter. "Weren't you supposed to be on duty tonight, Deputy Jones?"

Dallas stiffened. She didn't want to offer any more information than she had to. "Yes."

Sweeney straightened. "I heard ol' Harold Sims was hit by a sheriff's vehicle." Sweeney's brows rose. "Holy smokes! Was that you?"

Heat rose in Dallas's cheeks. She turned to Levi. "There's a couple of empty tables over there." She tipped her head in the direction of several empty tables. "How 'bout we take our drinks to one of them?"

Sweeney raised his hands in surrender. "Don't move on my account. I won't say another word. It's just that it's not often that a sheriff's deputy runs over a citizen of the county."

Levi pushed to his feet and glared at the bartender. He tossed a twenty on the counter and turned his back on Sweeney to face Dallas. "Ready to go?"

Sweeney touched his finger to his chin and stared up at the ceiling. "What's that motto again? *To serve and protect?* Harold was a good guy," Sweeney said. "A drunk, but a good guy."

Dallas didn't respond. She got up from her stool, left her beer on the counter and walked toward the door.

Levi cupped her elbow and walked alongside her. He didn't say a word.

A few men at the tables in the bar heard Sweeney, and all eyes followed Dallas as she left Sweeney's Bar.

When she got outside, she drew in a deep breath of the fresh night air.

"Let it go," Levi said. "Sweeney's a jerk."

She released the air in her lungs. "I didn't need the beer anyway," Dallas said. "A good cup of coffee would be better right now." She glanced over at him. "Truck stop?"

Levi's lips twisted. "Don't take this as hitting on you, but I make a pretty darn good cup of coffee, and my place is just around the corner. The best part about going there is that you don't have to face anybody else."

She nodded. "Or I could just go home and fix my own cup of coffee."

He shrugged. "Yes, you could."

"Want to join me?" she asked.

"I'd like that." Levi shook his head. "Though I set out to spend this evening alone, I realized I didn't really want to. Thanks," he said.

Dallas felt kind of silly climbing into two different vehicles again, but she didn't want to leave hers and didn't want him having an excuse to stay the night at her house because she was too lazy to take him back to his vehicle.

It wasn't a date.

It was just a cup of coffee.

The only thing Levi and Brian had in common was that they had both been in the army. Where Levi had been a Delta Force operative, Brian had been a truck driver carrying supplies between outposts. Both jobs were equally important in the army. Without the truck drivers, the supplies didn't get to the soldiers who needed them to fuel the battle and their bellies. The supply chain brought the beans and the bullets.

She drove the few blocks to her little cottage on the edge of town. It was a quiet street with mostly old people living in the houses beside or across from hers. Behind her was a large farmer's field. She assessed her cottage.

It had three small bedrooms and one small bathroom, but it was enough for her. She had rented it with the option to purchase if she ended up staying in Whiskey Gulch. After running over one of their own, the townsfolk would probably chase her away with torches and pitchforks. Never mind *he'd* stepped out in front of *her*. She'd been the only one to witness it. If the medical examiner's evidence didn't corroborate her statement, she could be in trouble.

She stared at the powder blue house with the white trim she'd fallen in love with on sight, and her chest tightened. She'd only been in Whiskey Gulch for a few months. It was far enough away from everything she had ever had with Brian. Being here was supposed to have been her new start.

Dallas drew in a deep breath and climbed out of her vehicle. She waited for Levi to join her. Then she climbed up the steps to the front door. The best feature and charm of the house was the huge front porch with hanging swings on either end. The house might be small, but the porch made up for it. She had sat there a couple of nights, waving at her neighbors before she got into her uniform and went to work. The place had felt like a home, something she hadn't had since before the deployment in which Brian had died.

She fumbled with the key and dropped it on the wood decking.

Before she could bend to retrieve the key ring, Levi scooped it up and stuck the house key into the doorknob with a frown. "No dead bolt?"

She shrugged. "Didn't seem necessary in such a small town."

"This small town has seen a murder and human trafficking in the past couple of months. Do yourself a favor and put in a dead bolt on both the front and the back doors, if you don't already have them."

She pushed the door open. "Seeing as I now have time, I might just do that…if I'm not job hunting."

"Surely the sheriff won't let you go."

She shrugged. "I'm the only one who saw what happened."

"Yeah, but the location of the dent on your car is evidence enough. You attempted to miss him."

She nodded and headed straight for the kitchen. "I can make coffee, or we could have those beers. I have a couple of cold ones in the refrigerator."

"Actually, coffee sounds good." He smiled. "Although, if *you* want something cold, I can understand after driving around in an un-air-conditioned truck in Texas." He cocked an eyebrow. "Why is it you drive around in an antique pickup? Surely they pay you enough to afford a newer ride with air-conditioning and electric windows and door locks."

Dallas's mouth twisted. "It's the sentimental value of the vehicle. I had a newer-model Jeep. It's hard to move around with two vehicles, so I chose the one that meant the most and sold the other."

"Understandable," he said with a slight nod. "Was it your father's or grandfather's?"

She turned to fish a filter and coffee grounds out of the cabinet above the sink. With her back to him, she answered, "No, it was my fiancé's. He left all his worldly goods to me."

For a moment, silence stretched between them. Then Levi spoke softly. "I'm so sorry for your loss."

"Yeah, well, that's the army for you. Doesn't matter what MOS you are. If you're deployed to a war zone, you're at risk. There's no clear enemy line."

"No, there isn't," he agreed. "What happened?"

She fit the filter in the coffee maker and scooped grounds into it. "You know…supply convoy meets IED. One minute everything's fine and you're planning a wedding. The next minute you're holding parts of your fiancé in your arms." Her back still to him, she pressed the start button on the coffee maker, then turned toward the refrigerator. "I've got some cheese and crackers if you'd like some."

"Thanks. That would be nice. I didn't have dinner."

Finally, she turned to face him and frowned. "I have some leftover pizza if you'd rather have that? If you don't eat it, it would probably just go bad in the refrigerator."

"Since you put it that way—" he grinned "— sure, but let me help."

"The plates are in the cabinet to the left of the sink." She reached into the refrigerator and pulled out a cardboard pizza box.

Levi found the plates and took out two and carried them to the table.

"I could nuke the pizza in the microwave," she said, "or I could warm up the oven and we could have it nice and crispy. Your choice."

"I've eaten cold pizza and been fine with that. I don't want you to have to go to any more trouble than you want to. I'll leave it up to you."

"Then oven it is." She turned on the switch for the oven and waited for the pilot light to ignite. While it heated, she slid the pizza onto a pan.

Levi found the coffee mugs and set them on the counter beside the coffee maker.

Every time they moved, they almost ran into each other. Her small kitchen wasn't big enough for two people unless those two people were comfortable being intimate.

Her heart fluttered at the thought. She hadn't felt any kind of attraction for another man since Brian's death. Why now? And why this Delta? Was it because he had been nice to her?

It hadn't been instant attraction between her and Brian. She'd met him at one of the bars outside of Fort Hood, Texas. They'd talked and exchanged names, but nothing more. After that night, he'd been sure to say hello to her at the gate when she pulled guard duty.

They'd been friends first. She'd liked that. No angsty feelings, sexual stress or being uncomfortable around him. She wasn't even sure when they'd gone from being friends to lovers. It had probably happened one night when they'd been watching TV together. They'd probably fallen asleep in each other's arms.

Their relationship certainly hadn't been instant attraction like she was feeling for Levi.

The man exuded masculinity. Since being with him, she felt safe and disturbed all at once. Having him so close in her kitchen stirred up feelings she'd never had with Brian, which she found extremely disconcerting.

"Why don't you sit down?" she said. "I'll take care of the rest."

He shook his head. "I didn't come here to be a bother."

"It's no bother," she insisted, needing him to get out of her way before she touched him once again. "It keeps me busy."

"If you insist." He took a seat at the small dinette table.

The table was a throwback from the fifties with its metal legs and a speckled top. The chair cushions were covered in shiny red vinyl. The kitchen cabinets needed updating, but Dallas kind of liked the retro style. It fit with the dinette. Fortunately, the house had come furnished. If she stayed, she'd probably replace some of the living room furniture. The retro style was okay but worn-out cushions weren't.

"Your first name's Dallas, isn't it?" Levi asked.

She nodded, pouring two cups full of coffee.

"Does the name have any special meaning for your parents?"

She snorted softly. "It meant something to my father. He was a traveling salesman. Dallas had been his most recent assignment when my mother went into labor. I suspect Dallas was also where his last lover was before I was born. There were many others after my birth and until my mother divorced him."

"Ouch," Levi said.

Dallas put the cups of coffee on the table, slid the pizza into the warm oven and set the timer. "It's okay. My mother and I did fine by ourselves. She wised up to his philandering ways and went back to school while they were still married. He paid for her education. She got a degree in nursing, and when she landed a good job, she filed for divorce."

Levi smiled. "She was a smart woman."

"Yes, she was." Her smile faded.

"I take it she's not with you anymore?"

"The irony was that she worked for an oncology clinic."

"Let me guess…" Levi's lips pressed together. "She died of cancer."

"She died of breast cancer while I was stationed in Germany." Dallas shook her head. "I flew back in time to say my goodbyes. I wish I'd been with her throughout her treatments. But she didn't tell me until near the end." She slid into the seat opposite Levi and sipped from her coffee cup.

"I'm sorry for your losses." He frowned. "That has to be really tough to lose the people you love."

"Yeah." She took another sip from her cup, then pinned him with her gaze. "You said tonight was your wedding anniversary. That has to be hard." She glanced into her mug. "Do you miss her?" Dallas held her breath waiting for his answer.

He hesitated for a moment before answering, "Yes and no." He gave a twisted smile. "I miss the idea of being married, of having someone to come home to after I've deployed, but I don't miss someone who doesn't miss me."

"Did she go into the marriage knowing that you were joining the army and would be a Delta Force operative?" Dallas asked.

"She knew I was going into the army. She wasn't very happy when I told her. I guess she was okay with it, at first. But like with everything I do, I do my best. Being a member of the army wasn't any different. I had to be the best of the best. Everything I did, I did to get better at my chosen career. She signed up for me to be in the army, but not for me to be gone all the time. She wanted me to get out, but I had worked too hard to become a Delta to walk away from it."

Dallas raised her eyebrows. "But you did."

"Yes, I did. I had agreed to get out in hope of salvaging my marriage. By the time I got home, though, it was over. She had already moved out of our house and in with her lover."

"Wow, that's harsh," Dallas said.

He shrugged. "I guess you could say I deserved it."

"Why didn't you go back on active duty?"

"I had committed to getting out and starting a life outside of the army."

"In other words, you don't like admitting to your mistakes."

He shook his head with a wry grin. "When you put it like that, I suppose you're right. Maybe I wanted to see what was so great about not being a Delta Force operative."

Dallas shook her head. "And here you are in Whiskey Gulch, Texas, drinking coffee with a broken-down cop."

He lifted his mug. "Here's to two broken-down former military people."

She touched the rim of her mug to his and took a long sip. "This beats beer anytime."

He nodded. "Yes, it does."

The oven alarm beeped.

Dallas set her mug on the table and rose to remove the pizza from the oven. The smell of bread, cheese and tomato sauce filled the air. For the first time that day, Dallas was actually hungry. She laid a hot pad on the middle of the table, carried the pizza pan from the oven and placed it on the middle of the hot pad.

Since Levi had already set the plates on the table, all Dallas had to do was to sit across from him and take a slice of pizza from the tray. After one bite she leaned back in her chair. "I believe this pizza is better the second time around."

Levi swallowed a bite. "I think it's the company that makes it so good."

Dallas nodded. "Thank you for taking my mind off the events of the evening. Even if for just a short time."

She had just taken another bite when the sound of something hitting the front of her house jerked her head up, and she heard breaking glass. Dallas jumped from her chair and ran toward the front door.

Levi caught up with her and passed her, his boots crunching on something beneath his feet.

Dallas switched on the light in the living room to find glass all over the wooden floor and one of the curtains billowing in the breeze. "What the heck?"

She reached for the front doorknob and would have yanked it open, but Levi laid his hand over hers. "You don't know what's out there. Let me go around the back and see if I can catch whoever broke your window."

"I'm the cop," Dallas said. "I'll do that."

"Sweetheart, you're the target. They may want to lure you out so that they can shoot you." He gripped her arms and looked down into her eyes. "Stay here. I'll be right back."

"I don't want you shot on my watch," she said.

"That's not gonna happen," he said. "Do you promise to stay?" His gaze gripped hers.

She nodded. "I'll stay."

Another rock sailed through a second window, shattering it and spraying glass all over the living room floor.

Dallas stiffened, her lips pressing tightly together. "Go get 'em."

Levi ran back to the kitchen and out through the back door.

Dallas stood away from the window and waited for the all-clear sign, hating that Levi was the one taking the initiative, not her. She was an officer of the law. Whoever was lobbing rocks at her windows should be stopped, and she should be the one to do it. Moments later, she heard a woman scream. Unable to hold back another minute, she yanked open the door and ran outside.

Levi had Ouida Sims by the arm. In her captured hand, she held a rock. She saw Dallas and screamed, "You killed my husband!"

Chapter Three

"Let go of me!" Mrs. Sims screamed.

"I'm sorry, ma'am," Levi said. "I can't let go of you until you drop that rock and pull yourself together."

The distraught woman caught sight of Dallas again and screamed, "Murderer! You killed him! You ran over my husband!"

"Ma'am, I think you need to listen to what the deputy's got to say," Levi said in a calm, clear tone. "I'm pretty sure that's not how it happened."

"I heard it. The news is all over town. She killed my husband." The woman's body went limp in his arms, and she shook with the force of her sobs. "She killed my husband," she whimpered, her voice choked with tears. "Harold's dead. The only man I ever cared about is gone. And it's all her fault." She turned and jabbed her finger at Dallas.

"Mrs. Sims—" Dallas stepped down from the porch "—I'm so sorry for your loss, but I did everything I could to miss him. He ran out in front of my vehicle. I couldn't stop fast enough."

"Harold's gone," Mrs. Sims said. "Harold's gone." She turned and buried her face in Levi's shirt and cried. He wrapped his arms around her and held her while she gave way to her grief, soaking the front of his shirt with her tears.

Dallas crossed to where Levi held the grieving woman. She reached out and touched her arm.

The widow flinched away. "Don't touch me. You…you…murderer."

Dallas dropped her arms to her sides. "I was on my way out to the Thatcher Ranch. I was still a couple miles from the turnoff at the big S curve in the road, when all of a sudden, Harold stepped out. Well, he staggered out into my path. I tried to stop. In fact, I turned the wheel and hit my brakes so hard I skidded sideways."

Ouida's shoulders shook harder, and her sobs grew louder.

Dallas stared over the woman's shoulder into Levi's gaze, shaking her head.

What could they do? There was no talking to the traumatized woman until she stopped crying.

Levi continued to hold her, letting her cry until she couldn't cry anymore.

After several minutes, her sobs slowly subsided. She lifted her head, gulped and turned toward Dallas. "Did he suffer?"

Dallas shook her head. "I didn't get a pulse. I tried to revive him. I did CPR until the EMTs arrived. But, Mrs. Sims… Ouida…when he staggered out in front of me, he already had blood on his face."

Ouida frowned. "Before you ran over him?"

Dallas nodded. "Yes. He lurched out into that road." Dallas's brow dipped. "He was so far away from the Thatcher Ranch, I didn't expect anyone to be on the road that late. Not there. Was there anything else that he would have done out in that direction?"

Ouida shook her head, and her eyes narrowed. "He did mention that a fence was down and that he might have to round up some of the cattle. Do you suppose he was injured by one of the cows?"

"I really don't know," Dallas said. "Hopefully the medical examiner can shed some light on that."

Ouida sniffed and swallowed hard. "All I know is he was going out to check the fences and the animals. He was supposed to be back for dinner. I was worried." Her eyes filled with more tears. "He asked me if I wanted to go with him. I should have gone. Maybe if I had, he wouldn't be dead now." More tears spilled down her face.

Dallas reached for the woman, and she fell into her arms.

Levi's chest was tight. The woman's pain was palpable. He wished there was more he could do to help her through it. "Ma'am, would you like to come inside and sit down?"

"I should go home," she said, the words garbled by yet another sob. "Oh, Lord. My home will be so empty now that Harold won't be there. I had his dinner ready. A plate set on the table…"

"Come inside, Mrs. Sims," Dallas begged. "I just brewed a fresh pot of coffee. If you don't like that, I think I have some tea in my cabinet."

The woman let Dallas lead her up the stairs and into the house.

Levi followed, stopping just inside the front door. "Where's your broom?" he asked as he stepped into the living room.

Dallas glanced over her shoulder. "In the front coat closet."

He opened the closet door, retrieved the broom and a dustpan and went to work cleaning up the glass. By the time he had finished and carried the dustpan into the kitchen to the trash, both women were sitting at the table with cups of coffee in front of them.

Dallas had her hand over Ouida's. "Mrs. Sims—"

Ouida shook her head. "Please, call me Ouida."

Dallas gave a brief smile. "Then you should call me Dallas."

Ouida gave her a watery smile. "I can't think of you as anything but Deputy Jones."

"Friends call each other by their first names," Dallas said. "I hope we can be friends, despite what happened."

Ouida's eyes filled again. "He's really gone, isn't he?"

Dallas squeezed her hand.

The sadness in her eyes made Levi's heart squeeze hard in his chest. Levi dumped the glass into the trash container, retrieved his coffee mug and topped it off with fresh hot coffee. He took his seat beside Dallas at the table. "Mrs. Sims, is there anybody that would have a grudge against your husband?"

She shook her head. "No. He was an alcoholic, but he'd quit drinking. He didn't owe anybody any money, and when he was drunk, he was a happy drunk, not belligerent. He just couldn't handle his booze. That didn't make him a bad man." She blinked and looked up at Levi. "Why? Do you think somebody hurt him? Do you think that's why he staggered out in front of Deputy Jones's car?"

Levi shrugged. "We won't know anything

more until the medical examiner has a chance to look at your husband's body."

Mrs. Sims's face screwed up again and more tears slid down her cheeks. "If he was chasing an animal that was loose, he would have been on one of the four-wheelers. Do you think he could have been tossed? Maybe wrecked the vehicle?"

Dallas nodded. "It's a possibility."

"Do you have any idea where the break in the fence was on the Thatcher Ranch?" Levi asked.

Ouida shook her head. "No, but my Harold would have taken one of the four-wheelers around all of the perimeter of the Thatcher Ranch to find the gap. He took his job seriously. Caring for the Thatcher Ranch while they're out of town was his way of proving himself after being released from rehab."

"Mrs. Sims," Levi said, "when are the Thatchers supposed to be back from Mexico?"

She pressed a hand to her mouth. "Tomorrow. If they had gotten back today, this wouldn't have happened. My Harold would be home, safe and alive."

"Do you happen to have the Thatchers' phone number or someplace where we can reach them?"

Ouida nodded, then pulled her cell phone out of her back pocket. She scrolled through her contacts list until she found Rafter T Ranch. Then she handed her phone to Levi.

He sent the number to his cell phone and saved it as a new contact.

"Ouida," Dallas said, "do you have any family close by or any close friends who can come stay with you tonight?"

She shook her head. "No, all I had was Harold."

Dallas smiled gently. "What about Mrs. Betsy Allen? I've seen you two have coffee together."

"Oh, yes, yes." Ouida waved a hand. "I forgot. She is a very good friend."

"Do you have her number?" Dallas asked.

She nodded her head toward the phone Levi still held. "In my contacts list."

Dallas shot a glance toward Levi.

Levi scrolled through Mrs. Sims's contacts list until he found Betsy Allen. "I'm going to call your friend Betsy," Levi said. "I'll see if she can come spend some time with you."

"Thank you," Ouida said. "I don't know what I would do without you two."

Levi didn't point out that she hadn't felt that way minutes before. He was just glad that she wasn't still throwing rocks at Dallas's windows. He dialed Mrs. Allen's number and waited several rings before the woman answered. "Betsy Allen, this is Levi Warren calling on behalf of

Ouida Sims. I'm sorry to say that her husband passed away tonight, and she needs a friend."

"Oh, dear Lord," Betsy Allen said. "Where is she? I'll be right there. Better yet, can you get her to my house? I can imagine she doesn't want to go home right now."

"I can do that, Mrs. Allen. Just give me your address."

The woman on the other end of the line gave Levi the address. Without anything to write on, he committed it to memory. "Thank you, Mrs. Allen. We'll bring her over in the next few minutes." He ended the call and stared across the table at Ouida Sims. "Betsy wants you to stay at her house tonight."

"I'll need to get a few things from mine," Ouida said.

"You tell us what you need, and we'll go in and get it for you," Levi said.

She nodded and let Dallas help her to her feet. "I don't know what I'm going to do."

Dallas slipped an arm around her waist. "You're going to Betsy Allen's house and stay the night with her. You don't need to be alone right now. You need to be with someone who knows you and loves you."

Ouida let Dallas guide her through the house and out the front door. "What about my car?" The woman waved a hand toward the sedan parked at an angle in the street. "I can't leave it here. I'll need it in the morning."

"Levi will drive you to Betsy Allen's place," Dallas said. "I'll drive your car and park it outside on her driveway."

Mrs. Sims nodded. "Thank you, Deputy— I mean, Dallas."

Dallas hugged her before she helped her up into Levi's truck. Then she stood back. "Wait," she said. "I need your keys."

Ouida dug in her pocket and came up empty. She shook her head. "I left them in the ignition."

The woman had been so distraught that Levi wasn't surprised she'd left the keys in her car. Levi frowned and paused before getting into the driver's seat. "Are you going to be all right, Dallas?"

She nodded. "I'll be right behind you."

He climbed behind the driver's wheel and waited for Dallas to go back and lock the door to her house and then climb into Ouida Sims's vehicle. When Dallas gave him a thumbs-up, Levi pulled out into the street and drove the few blocks to Betsy Allen's place.

All the lights shone from the windows and the front porch. Mrs. Allen came out in her bathrobe.

No sooner had he parked the truck than Levi could see Dallas jogging up beside the passenger side, opening it to help Ouida out onto the ground. She walked with the older woman up the front steps to where Mrs. Betsy Allen waited with open arms.

Levi followed.

Ouida fell into her friend's embrace and sobbed quietly.

Dallas laid a hand on the woman's back and looked at Betsy over Ouida's shoulder. "I've got the keys to her house. I can go get the things that she needs."

"Don't worry about it," Mrs. Allen said. "I have an extra nightgown, toothbrush, brush and a robe all set aside. Everything else we can get tomorrow, unless she has some medications she needs."

Ouida shook her head. "I don't."

"If you need anything for a headache or to help you go to sleep, I have items in my medicine cabinet," Mrs. Allen said.

Ouida nodded. "Thank you, dear."

Dallas held out the keys to Ouida's car.

Mrs. Allen took them. "Thank you for getting her here, Deputy Jones."

"Yes, ma'am. Let me know if you two need anything. Don't hesitate to call."

Levi turned with Dallas and headed back to his truck. She slipped into the passenger side while he climbed behind the wheel.

Dallas didn't say anything on the trip back to her cottage. When they arrived, Levi shifted into Park.

Dallas sat staring through the window without moving.

"Are you all right?" he asked.

She shook her head. "I need to know what happened." She turned toward Levi. "Why was Harold Sims so far away from the Thatcher Ranch? Why did he have blood on his face? Why did he stagger out in front of me?"

"The sheriff will conduct his investigation," Levi said.

"Speaking of the sheriff, take me to the sheriff's department." She shook her head as if having a second thought. "Never mind, I'll take my own vehicle."

Levi reached across and grabbed her arm. "Let me take you," he said. "We've come this far together."

She relaxed back against the seat. "Thank you. You don't know how much I appreciate that."

He backed out onto the street again and drove to the sheriff's department.

The sheriff's vehicle was out front. When they walked through the door, they found the sheriff talking on the phone. He nodded, acknowledging their presence, and held up a finger as he spoke into the receiver. "Glad he made it. We hope to know something by tomorrow, if at all possible…" the sheriff said. "I know, but anything you can tell me might help in this investigation. The sooner the better. Thank you, Dr. Morrison." He ended the call and placed his cell phone in his pocket.

"Have you heard anything new?" Dallas asked.

He shook his head. "No. Harold Sims's body just made it to the medical examiner. Dr. Morrison said he'd get to him first thing in the morning."

Dallas frowned. "Did you find anything at the scene of the accident?"

The sheriff shook his head. "No. I put in a request for the state crime scene investigation team. Hopefully they'll get here at first light." He shook his head. "I know it's not much, but I believe what you told me."

Dallas laughed, but the sound was hollow. "Thank you, sir. Let's hope a judge and a jury feel the same."

"Don't you worry, Deputy Jones." The sheriff touched her arm. "We'll clear you. In the meantime, you're not to investigate this case."

She shook her head. "Sheriff, I know this department is shorthanded. You barely have enough people to patrol."

The sheriff's lips tightened. "We'll manage."

Levi stepped forward. "You know, if you need any help, my boss, Trace Travis, may be willing to provide assistance."

The sheriff's brow furrowed. "How so?"

"He's hired me and some other former military guys for his organization called the Outriders. His plan is to use us as another line of defense to help people in need." Levi tipped his head toward Dallas. "Seems like your deputy is in need of protection and assistance."

The sheriff frowned. "She can't be involved in this investigation."

Levi nodded. "I understand, but what about me?"

The sheriff's eyes narrowed. "I'd have to perform a background check on you. If it comes back good, I'd have to deputize you. Who do I contact? Just you? Or do I need to touch base with Trace Travis?"

Levi squared his shoulders. "Me, but I'll have Trace Travis give you a call. I'm sure he'll have no problem. I'm waiting on my first assignment anyway. Also, I had a top secret clearance in the army." He grinned. "And I'm kind of tired of mucking stalls."

"I gotta admit, it's tempting," the sheriff said. "As it is, I'm having to pull this night shift. I couldn't get anybody else to come in."

"I'm so sorry, Sheriff," Dallas said.

The older man shook his head. "It's not your fault. We just have to prove that. In the meantime, I have a department to run, a shift to fill and an investigation to manage. The crime scene investigation team might be of some assistance. At the very least, they'll gather evidence at the scene, and they'll look at the vehicle as well. You two should go home and get some rest. Tomorrow will be a full day trying to figure this mess out."

"Thank you, Sheriff." Dallas popped a salute.

"We'll see you tomorrow." Levi stepped out of the sheriff's office and held the door for Dallas.

She shook her head. "You know, I'm fully capable of opening my own door."

He smiled. "Call me old-fashioned. I open doors for people, male or female."

She nodded. "In that case, thank you."

Levi drove her back to her house and parked in front on the driveway.

She turned to him. "Thank you, Levi. You made a very unpleasant evening a little easier to bear."

He nodded. "Let me walk you up to your door and make sure that everything's okay. You have a couple of broken windows. I can stick around and board them up."

She shook her head. "No, that won't be necessary. If anybody wants to break in, I'll hear more shattering glass. Besides, I sleep with my .45 on the pillow beside me."

He chuckled. "Remind me not to kiss you good-night, if you're not fully awake."

Her cheeks turned pink in the light from the dash. She ducked her head and pushed open the door.

He got out and ran around to the other side, but she was already down, her feet on the ground.

"You really do take that chivalry thing to the next level, don't you?" she said.

Levi puffed out his chest and smiled. "My mama taught me right."

"Thank her for me," Dallas said with a grin. "She did good."

His smile faded. "That would be difficult, since she's passed away."

Dallas's brow dipped. "I'm sorry. I didn't know that."

"So, we have one more thing in common. We've both lost our mothers."

"You said *one more thing*," Dallas pointed out. "What else?"

"Coffee at midnight and leftover pizza."

"You're right. We're practically twins." She slipped her key into the lock and turned it. "Thanks, again."

He rested his hand over hers. "Please, let me

just go in and check that everything's okay. I swept up the glass. I want to make sure I got it all."

"Thank you for doing it. You didn't have to," she said.

"Maybe not, but I'm glad I did." He glanced down at her boots. "Wouldn't want your bare feet all cut up."

"True," she said. She stepped back and waved her hand. "Go ahead."

He slipped through the door and made a quick perusal of all the rooms in the house, ensuring nobody had come in while they were gone. When he was certain it was safe, he returned to her at the front door. "Are you sure you don't want me to nail some boards over the broken windows?"

She shook her head. "No, the broken glass will give me enough warning, and I don't expect anybody to try to break in."

"You didn't expect anybody to throw rocks through your windows. And now you have two broken windows."

She nodded. "Good point, but I'm a light sleeper, especially since this was supposed to be my night to work. I'll just stay up and watch TV most of the time anyway."

"If I get the sheriff's full buy-in tomorrow, I want to go out to the Thatcher Ranch, see if there's any clues as to what happened to Harold Sims. His wife said he was going out to check on some fences that might be down. We might want to start there, since he ended up off the ranch."

"We?" Dallas raised her eyebrows.

He raised his eyebrows, too. "You're coming with me, aren't you?"

She looked at him with her eyes narrowing. "I'm off the case. I'm not supposed to investigate. You heard the sheriff."

"So, you won't investigate. You can leave that to me." He touched a hand to his chest. "However, you can play tour guide and show me how to get there. Remember, I'm new to this place."

A smile spread across her face. "I like the way you think."

"I find I'm liking your company. Beats wallowing in self-pity on my anniversary," he said.

She nodded. "You've got that right. If the sheriff buys in, what time shall we begin?"

"I muck stalls in the morning," Levi said. "I can pick you up at eight."

"I'll be ready." She leaned up and kissed his cheek. "Thank you again." She ducked into the house, closed the door and locked it behind her.

Levi lifted a hand to his cheek where she'd kissed him. Heat spread from that point throughout his face, down his neck and throughout the rest of his body. Having just signed divorce papers, his feelings for the cute deputy were unexpected, and he hadn't felt anything like them in the last couple of years of his marriage.

He'd hung in with CeCe, thinking that all marriages aged to the point where the flame had burned into complacency and respect. He'd foolishly thought that that was good enough.

Then a deputy sheriff landed one innocent thank-you kiss on his cheek and stirred something inside of him that he didn't think he could extinguish, nor did he want to.

Levi slowly drove away, wondering if he should stay and camp out in front of her house just to make sure nobody broke in. Then he remembered she was a fully capable MP and a sheriff's deputy. The woman knew how to use a gun, and she wasn't afraid to. He drove to the little house he'd rented, two blocks off Main Street, parked in the drive and entered through the front door. He was glad Dallas had insisted on having coffee at her house. If they had come to his, he had the coffee, but he didn't have much furniture to speak of, just his gun safe and his recliner, along with a couple of outside folding chairs that he'd brought in from the storage shed.

He stripped, showered, dried off and lay naked on his bed, wishing the air conditioner could keep up with the Texas heat. All the while he thought about Dallas Jones, wondering what she was thinking about at that moment.

Was she asleep? Would she have nightmares? Hell, he bet she had nightmares already just from watching her fiancé die in her arms. Now, having been somewhat responsible for the death of a civilian, she had to be churning the incident over and over in her mind.

He thought about calling her, and then realized that he didn't have her phone number, nor had she asked for his. He'd remedy that tomorrow. In the meantime, he needed to get some sleep. Although, he wasn't sure how he'd do that, not with the tingling sensation in his cheek where she'd kissed him. He lay in bed counting the minutes until eight o'clock the next morning.

Chapter Four

Dallas spent the night tossing and turning, going over everything that had happened that evening. From Ouida asking her to look out for Harold, to hitting Harold and, finally, the impetuous kiss she'd planted on Levi's cheek.

After all he'd done for her…holy hell. Had she really kissed the man? What had come over her?

She didn't fall asleep until somewhere around four o'clock in the morning. When she did drift off, she was plagued by nightmares of the IED explosion that had ended the lives of six soldiers. The tragedy played over and over in her mind like a film on a continuous loop.

This time when she bent to take Brian in her arms, it wasn't Brian's face she saw, but Levi's handsome one. The man she barely knew and had kissed that night.

Dallas was glad when her alarm went off at six, freeing her of the nightmare and the guilt it had instilled. Levi was not the man she'd loved and promised to marry. He was just a guy who had happened across an accident scene and stayed with her to make sure she was all right.

Perhaps she'd been so traumatized that her subconscious clung to Levi as rescuer, which was ridiculous. She was not the type of woman who needed rescuing. She was the type who rescued others.

Well, she certainly hadn't rescued Harold Sims. The man lay somewhere in the medical examiner's office being picked apart. Her heart hurt for the man and his wife. She hoped they'd find clues that would reveal what had happened to him before he'd stepped in front of her vehicle.

And she hoped those clues would clear her of any wrongdoing.

She made a mental note to check on Ouida Sims that day. The woman had been so distraught the night before. Though Dallas knew she couldn't have done anything differently, she still felt a load of guilt. The man was dead because she had run over him. Whether she was at fault or not, it didn't change those facts.

She performed her morning calisthenics, sit-ups, push-ups and stretches. And then went for her usual two-mile run. The fresh air helped clear her mind. The exercise helped to relieve the tension. When she returned to her cottage, she heard a voice call out from across the street.

"Ms. Jones."

She turned to find Ruth Miller standing on her front porch, her hair perfectly combed, makeup on and dressed precisely. The woman never stepped out of her house unless she looked her best. At seventy-nine years old, she managed to get out twice a day and walk two miles each time, which was a lot more than most people her age could do.

"Good morning, Mrs. Miller," she said with a smile.

"Thought I heard some commotion out here last night. Everything okay?"

"Yes, ma'am," Dallas responded. She didn't see the need to go into any of the details about having run over a man the night before, or that the man's wife had come to throw rocks in her windows. By noon, Ruth would have the whole story. She was the kind of woman who cared about everyone in the neighborhood. Caring meant that she also knew everybody's business.

"If you need anything, you let me know," she said.

"Thank you, ma'am. I will."

She tipped her head toward Dallas's cottage. "I know the man at the glass shop. Want me to give you his name and number?"

"That would be really helpful," Dallas said. Nothing got by that woman. She made for a good neighborhood watch.

"Well, have a good day," Ruth said.

"Yes, ma'am. You, too."

"Oh, and, Deputy Jones," Ruth called out.

"Yes, ma'am?"

"If you need someone to talk to, I'm here."

A lump lodged in Dallas's throat. The woman truly cared. She'd seen others of her neighbors sitting on Ruth's porch. Ruth carried food to those who'd suffered tragedies, as if food could mend everything. Sometimes, it really helped.

Dallas glanced at her watch. Shoot, she only had a few minutes to get showered, dressed and ready for when Levi would show up at eight o'clock.

"Talk to you later, Mrs. Miller." She ran into her house, stripped off her clothes and jumped into the shower. A few minutes later she was dry, except for her hair, which she slicked back into a ponytail at the nape of her neck. It made her look a bit austere, but she really didn't care how she looked. Not much, anyway, and she had high cheekbones, so she could pull it off. She'd just finished tying her shoes when she heard the rumble of an engine pulling up in her driveway.

Her heart fluttered, and she shoved her cell phone and her wallet in her back pocket, slipped her shoulder holster over her arms and a jacket over that. Then she ran to the door.

She wasn't excited about the man coming to pick her up. No, sir. She wanted to get on with the investigation.

Or so she told herself.

By the time she pulled open the door, her neighbor Ruth was in the driveway talking with Levi. She held a note in her hand.

Ruth glanced up at Dallas. "Oh, there she is." Ruth smiled and waved. "I was just talking to your young man."

Dallas stopped beside Levi's truck and stared up at the ATV in the back with the sheriff's department logo emblazoned on the side.

Dallas cocked an eyebrow. "How'd you get that?"

"The sheriff loaned it to me," he said.

Good. The man was obviously thinking ahead.

"He's not my young man," Dallas said.

Ruth ignored Dallas's remark and held out the sheet of paper. "I brought you the name and number of the glass man here in Whiskey Gulch. He should be able to replace your windows quickly. He had mine fixed the same day I called him. The lawn mower threw a rock up into mine. I'd never had that happen before, and I'd never used that lawn service before, either.

I used to do all my mowing myself, until my confounded mower broke. I figured it was time to let somebody else take care of my lawn." Ruth took a breath and sighed. "I miss those days. There's something relaxing about going back and forth across your lawn. And I love the smell of cut grass." She frowned and blinked. "Weren't you on night shift this week?"

Dallas sighed. "I was. I'm not now."

"I can't believe they put you on administrative leave. Anybody who knows you knows you wouldn't have run over Harold Sims on purpose. You don't have a mean bone in your body. That's what I was just telling Mr. Warren. He agrees."

Dallas held her tongue. How could Mr. Warren possibly know anything about her when he'd only known her for all of a handful of hours?

"Mr. Warren says you two are going out in the country today." Ruth's face broke out in a sunny smile. "Are you going to do some horseback riding?"

Dallas met Levi's gaze. His lips were twitching at the corners. "I don't know what we're doing."

Ruth patted Levi on the arm. "I'm sure Mr. Warren has everything planned."

He nodded, his face serious, the hint of a smile wiped from his face. "Yes, ma'am, I do."

"Isn't that nice." She stared up at Levi and actually batted her eyes. "Is this your first date, then?"

Dallas frowned. "It's not a date. Just two people going out in the country."

Ruth grinned broadly. "On a date."

Dallas's frown deepened. "It's not a date."

"Well, that's what we called it when I was your age. When two unmarried people go out together, it's a date." Ruth's brow furrowed. "What are they calling it now? Am I not keeping up with the times?"

Levi winked. "It's a date."

Ruth clapped her hands. "I knew it. Are you taking a picnic lunch?"

"I hadn't thought about that," Levi said. "I figured we'd come back through town and grab something at the diner."

"That'll be nice, too." Ruth raised a finger. "Although, if you plan ahead, they can have a picnic lunch ready for you."

Dallas gritted her teeth to keep from saying something snarky.

"Well, don't let me keep you from your date." Ruth backed away. "And don't forget to call the glass man."

"I won't, and thanks again, Ruth." Her neighbor really did mean well and was trying to take care of her. She took care of everyone else.

Ruth walked back across the street to her cottage.

Levi chuckled. "I like your neighbor."

Dallas smiled and waved at Ruth. "I do, too. She's like a mother hen for everyone else on the block."

Levi smiled and waved once more in Ruth's direction. "It's nice to know she's looking out for you."

"Yes, it is." Dallas turned her attention to Levi. "Ready?"

He cocked an eyebrow. "No issue with taking my truck?"

Dallas huffed. "No. Mine's pretty reliable, though, just for the record."

"I believe you. But I know mine better. I'm ready."

She nodded. "Let's go. I want to find out what happened to Harold Sims." She climbed into the truck beside Levi.

He shifted into gear and pulled out onto the street. "I had a chat with the sheriff earlier. My boss called him and offered my services. The sheriff had already run a background check on me through the criminal database."

Dallas raised her eyebrows. "And?"

"I came up clean, and he deputized me." With a grin, he pulled a sheriff's star out of his pocket. "I guess it's official. I'm a deputy."

Dallas's lips twisted. "I guess they'll let anybody be a deputy in this county. Maybe I should move to a big city where you actually have to have training in state and federal law and law enforcement."

"Hey, I've got training. I know how to fire twenty-some-odd different weapons."

She raised both hands. "Ooh, I feel safer already."

He laughed out loud. "You sure know how to stroke a guy's ego."

"I have a feeling yours doesn't need it," she said, her lips twitching.

"That's where you might be wrong."

She shot a quick glance in his direction. The man exuded confidence. Perhaps his divorce had set him back some. "Sorry," she said. "I really do appreciate your help and that you're letting me come along."

"Yeah, well, about that… When we're going down Main Street, you might want to duck down."

They'd just arrived at the stop sign where they'd turn left onto Main Street.

"Seriously?" Dallas leaned forward, tucking her head below the dash.

"Yeah. The last thing the sheriff said is that you couldn't be involved in the investigation. I think that's about the sixth time he's said that. He might just mean it."

As they drove south of town, Dallas studied the land, the shoulders of the road and the ditches, especially when they came to the S curve where she'd hit Harold Sims.

Several state government vehicles were parked alongside the road, their hazard lights flashing. Men and women wearing gloves scoured the ditches and the field beside the road.

More than anything, Dallas wanted to stop and ask them how it was going and if they'd found anything.

"I'll be sure to ask the sheriff what they found," Levi said, as if reading her mind.

"Thank you," she said. "I hate that I'm not supposed to be involved."

"Yeah, it's got to be hard," Levi said. "You have the most to lose if things go wrong."

Dallas shook her head. "No, I don't have the most to lose. Harold did, and he lost it."

"True," Levi said. "And I'm determined to find out why and who did it."

"Thanks," Dallas said. "There has to be something out there that gives us a clue as to why Harold Sims was here and not at the Rafter T Ranch."

"Well, while they're exploring this end of it," Levi said as he passed the cluster of vehicles and picked up speed, "we're going to the Rafter T Ranch and start there."

They continued on the way out to the Thatchers' ranch a couple more miles down the highway and turned in at the gate. Fortunately, it was only a cattle guard with no actual gate to open or close.

"The sheriff told me that he had contacted the Thatchers to let them know Harold Sims had passed away. He told them that if they planned to stay any longer, they might need to contact somebody to take care of the animals."

"How did the Thatchers take it?" Dallas asked.

"They were upset about the loss of Mr. Sims. Mr. Thatcher informed the sheriff that they would be home today, later on this afternoon. The sheriff also told the Thatchers that he was sending one of his deputies out to investigate to see if there were any other clues associated with Harold. The ranch owners gave their approval."

"That's nice to know. Otherwise, we would be trespassing," Dallas said.

"And how do you feel about trespassing?" Levi asked.

"I work hard not to break the law." She stared straight out the front windshield. "However, when my life and my career are on the line, I might bend a few rules."

"Good, because once we're on Thatcher land, if it leads off, we might be trespassing on someone else's property."

"I'd thought about that." Dallas chewed her bottom lip.

Dallas lifted a shoulder. "Sometimes, I find it's easier to beg forgiveness than to ask for permission. If we run into any other ranchers, we'll cross that bridge then. Ouida said that there was a fence down that Harold was going to check on."

"The problem with that is that the Rafter T Ranch is over six hundred acres. That damaged fence could be anywhere," Levi said. "We should probably aim for the north side since it's closest to where you found Harold."

"It could just as easily have been along the front, but I didn't see any fences down as we passed along the roadside."

Levi nodded. "Then perhaps we should look at the north and the west."

Dallas tipped her head toward the truck bed. "I'm glad you had the foresight to bring an ATV."

"I thought we might need it, and I didn't want to borrow the Thatchers' horses or vehicles."

She smiled across at him. "Are you sure you weren't a rancher in another life?"

He grinned. "Actually, I earned money dur-

ing the summertime working on a ranch while
I was in high school."

Dallas chuckled. "So, you're not completely
green."

Levi shook his head. "No, I'm not. I know
one end of a cow from another, and I ride horses
as well."

She crossed her arms over her chest and
grinned at him. "You really do have to be suc-
cessful at everything you attempt."

His lips twisted. "Don't think too highly of
me. I failed at marriage."

"You failed to choose the right woman," Dallas said. "You needed a woman who was more
independent. One who could stand being alone
for long periods of time and could handle it."

He chuckled. "You got someone in mind?"

"Not right off the top of my head. If you want
me to, I'll put my thinking cap on. I might come
up with the perfect match for you."

He raised one hand. "Whoa. I just got out of
a bad marriage. I don't want to get back into
another one too soon."

"It won't be a bad marriage if you marry the
right person."

Levi shot a glance her way. "Someone like
you?"

"Maybe," she said, her heart speeding up.

"But like you, I'm not in the market for a relationship."

"How long has your fiancé been gone?" he asked.

"Over two years."

"What is the appropriate amount of time to grieve, or is that an insensitive question?"

"I don't know." Dallas stared out the front windshield. "I guess as long as it takes."

He smiled at her. "You must have loved him."

She nodded. "He was my best friend. We were supposed to get married, raise two or three kids, travel the world and settle down somewhere to grow old."

"You know you're young enough," Levi said. "There's got to be someone else out there for you. Someone who wants the same things and can appreciate you for who you are. You're a pretty amazing woman."

Dallas shook her head. "I intimidate most men, and starting over in a new relationship scares the crap out of me."

"You shouldn't be afraid. You're a good, caring person. You deserve to have all those things you wanted, and I'd bet anything that you'd make a great mother."

She nodded. "I really wanted those kids."

"Then don't wait," Levi said. "Get back out there. Find someone to love."

Dallas had been having similar thoughts over the past few weeks, but moving on was hard. It was like losing Brian all over again.

Levi parked the truck in the barnyard and unloaded the ATV.

Dallas shivered in anticipation of riding double with him.

"You *are* taking me, aren't you?" she asked.

Levi blinked. "I wouldn't think of leaving you behind."

"Good, because you're not," she said.

They started by poking around the barn and the outbuildings. Then they made a circle around the main house. Nothing looked like the site of an altercation between Harold and someone else. Everything appeared as it should, neat and tidy. They found a few ATVs in the barn in one of the stalls, and there was room for one more.

Levi studied the four-wheelers. "If Harold had gone out to check fences, he would have taken an ATV or ridden a horse."

"I would guess that he would have taken an ATV versus a horse. The Thatchers are known for being pretty protective of their horseflesh. I hear they paid a lot of money for them and even more to have them trained."

"We'll assume that Harold took an ATV, and we'll look for one," Levi said.

They returned to the truck where the ATV stood.

Levi climbed on the front and patted the seat behind him. He held out a helmet.

Dallas slid the helmet over her head, buckled it beneath her chin and then climbed onto the back of the ATV.

"Hold on tight," Levi said as he started the engine and shifted into gear.

Once he'd driven out of the barnyard, Dallas dismounted long enough to open and close the gate to the pasture. Searching a six-hundred-acre ranch might be like trying to find a needle in a haystack. They just had to persevere and find the evidence they needed to solve the case she wasn't supposed to be investigating.

"You didn't have two of these things?" Dallas asked.

"Couldn't fit two in the back of the truck. Otherwise, I would have brought an extra." Levi grinned over his shoulder. "You have to admit, this is cozier. But don't worry… It's not a date."

As Dallas wrapped her arms around Levi's waist, she couldn't help the smile spreading across her face.

Chapter Five

After riding over several hills and down into gullies and ravines, Dallas called out, "Are you sure you know where you're going?"

"The four-wheeler's compass says we're headed north," he yelled over the sound of the engine. "I assume that's the direction in which we'll find the northern property fence."

She tightened her grip around his waist as he sent the ATV charging up a hill. She liked that his belly was tight and muscular. The man wasn't letting himself go since leaving active duty. She admired people who had the motivation and desire to stay fit. She wondered if he jogged. It would be nice to have someone with whom to run.

Dallas had heard that there was a good trail along the river. She hesitated to go alone, preferring to make her route through the streets of Whiskey Gulch. She remembered the woman who'd been attacked along the river trail. One of

Trace Travis's men had helped to solve that case. Because they had found one man who was attacking women didn't mean there weren't more. Though she knew some solid self- defense techniques, she didn't like risking her life with no backup.

When they topped the next rise, Dallas leaned around Levi. A small herd of cattle stood between them and a fence. Some of the animals had made their way to the other side through a break in the wire. She pointed to the gap.

Levi nodded and aimed the ATV in that direction, weaving his way between the cows and steers. Some bellowed their protest; others meandered out of the way. Half a dozen followed the four-wheeler, possibly hoping to be fed something other than the grass they were grazing on.

Once at the break in the fence, Levi parked the ATV, and they dismounted.

Dallas studied the area around the damaged fence.

Levi bent to check out the break. "This wire's been cut."

Dallas knelt beside some fencing tools, including a box of nails, a roll of barbed wire and a come-along.

Levi straightened and stared out across the

pasture on the other side of the fence. "He was here all right."

"Why would he leave his tools lying on the ground?" Dallas asked.

"Could be that he didn't want to fix the fence until he got the strays back on this side, which would explain why he'd taken his ATV through the break."

Dallas stood with her hands fisted on her hips, staring across the fence to the ranch beyond. "But where to?"

"Maybe we should follow the adventure-seeking cattle."

"How do we know they don't belong to the rancher on that side?" Dallas asked.

"Most of these cattle have a green tag on their ear. I would assume that the green tags mean that they belong to the Rafter T Ranch."

Dallas frowned. "Don't they brand cattle?"

Levi shrugged. "Sometimes, but it's easier to tag an ear. And it's less painful for the animal."

The cows that had followed them to the break in the fence mooed as if impatient for them to feed them.

Levi drove the four-wheeler to the other side. As a temporary measure, he and Dallas stretched the come-along between two fence posts to block the cattle from coming through.

"It isn't much, but hopefully it will deter some of them from crossing over," he reasoned.

The cows mooed but stayed on their side.

Levi and Dallas climbed on the back of the ATV and drove across the pasture of the neighboring ranch, following the line of cows that had found their way there, hoping they would lead in the direction Harold had taken the day before.

Dallas could only see what was out to the right or the left of Levi, but she couldn't see what was directly ahead of them with Levi's broad shoulders blocking her view. They followed the trail of cattle across the pasture, down into a ravine and back up the other side. A stand of trees obscured what lay beyond.

Levi slowed the ATV and drove along the edge of the woods until he found a path leading in.

At the head of the trail, Dallas noticed a pile of dung with an ATV track through the middle of it. Dallas's pulse picked up. "Could be Harold's."

Levi nodded and drove into the woods.

Overhanging branches dimmed the sunlight. Dallas leaned as far as she could around Levi to see what was ahead, watching for low-hanging branches. Eventually, the trees opened into a clearing where a ramshackle hut stood, with weathered wood and a tin roof. It couldn't have been more than a one-room cabin. Probably used by the ranchers for hunting. It appeared abandoned.

Levi slowed in front of the building. "Hello!" he yelled. "Anyone home?" He stopped. Dallas got off the back. Levi shifted into Neutral and set the parking brake, leaving the engine running. "Let me go first," he said.

"I'm just as capable as you are," she argued.

He smiled. "I know, but you're not supposed to be investigating."

Dallas acquiesced and followed behind Levi as he approached the cabin.

He stopped short and bent to study the dirt in front of the door.

Dallas looked over his shoulder to see a dark stain in the dirt. "Is that blood?"

"Looks like it to me," Levi said. He pulled his handgun from his shoulder holster. Then he stepped around the bloodstain, and using the hem of his T-shirt, he gently twisted the knob on the cabin door, careful not to disturb any fingerprints if any were there. He stood to the side and swept his hand out to guide her around behind him, then gently pushed open the door.

"I'm going in," he said. "I need you to stay out here to watch my back."

She nodded. "I've got you covered."

He eased into the cabin, disappearing into the dark. When he came back out, he had his shirt pulled up over his nose.

"What's wrong?" she asked, and then the aroma of eggs hit her. "Meth?"

He nodded, dropped the shirt from his face and drew in a deep breath of fresh air. "Definitely need to let the sheriff see this."

She looked around him into the dark interior of the cabin. "Anything of interest inside besides the smell?"

Levi shook his head. "Nothing but some empty boxes. It's been cleaned out."

"You think that's Harold's blood?"

Levi shrugged. "If not his, it's somebody else's. If it's Harold's, whoever caused his injury took off with his ATV. Or Harold took off on his ATV after being injured. Either way, we still haven't found Harold's wheels."

The sound of a small engine roared in the distance.

"We better leave before whoever is headed this way spots us," Levi said. "And the sooner we get the sheriff out here, the better. I have a feeling that what little evidence is left won't last long." Levi straddled the seat of the ATV, and Dallas climbed on behind him. He revved the engine and took off, heading for the closest line of trees in the opposite direction of the trail.

Levi focused on what was ahead of them; Dallas looked behind. As they entered the woods, a motorcycle blew into the clearing from the trail.

Dallas glanced over her shoulder and muttered a curse. "There's somebody back there!" she shouted.

"Are they armed?" Levi yelled over his shoulder.

"I don't know."

The motorcycle rider raised his hand, aiming a gun in their direction. A shot rang out.

"Go! Go! Go!" Dallas yelled. "He's shooting at us."

Levi raced through the woods, dodging trees right and left.

Dallas clung around his middle, praying they didn't hit a tree or that a bullet didn't hit them.

The motorcycle was better equipped to handle tight turns and was quickly catching up. Another one fell in behind him.

"Now there's two!" she yelled. "We can't outrun them. Find a place to ditch this ATV."

Levi drove to the bottom of the hill and followed a streambed to the west, kicking up water on both sides. When he came to a bend in the creek with a rocky outcropping hanging over the stream, he yelled out, "Be ready to jump."

On the other side of the overhang, he hit the

brakes, and before the ATV stopped rolling, he yelled, "Jump!"

Dallas bailed, rolled and took up a position on the other side of the rocks. Levi dived off the ATV and rolled to a stop beside her.

Dallas could hear the scream of a motorcycle racing up the creek bed.

She rose to a kneeling position, her weapon aimed toward the sound of the oncoming engine.

A motorcycle erupted around the corner.

Dallas took her time with her aim, not wanting to kill the guy and not wanting to be killed by him. A shot sounded from behind her.

The motorcycle turned sharply and then lay down and skidded in the gravel and water, blasting waves of water up on both sides. The bike's tire continued to spin even as the motorcycle came to a rest, but the rider lay still, submerged in the creek.

Another engine roared nearby.

Dallas waited for the rider to appear around the bend in the creek. The sound neared, but no bike appeared around the rock outcropping. The noise sounded as if it were right on top of them.

Dallas cast a glance skyward to the bluff above the creek.

A motorcycle rumbled above them, the rider aiming his gun down at her and Levi.

Levi still aimed at the creek, waiting for the other bike to roar around the bend.

Dallas rolled onto her back and fired a shot at the man hovering over them. His shoulder jerked back from the impact of the bullet, and he swayed. Then he raised his hand, aiming his weapon again at Dallas. She fired off another round, this time hitting the man square in the chest. He fell forward. Rider and bike slid over the edge of the cliff.

"Watch out!" Dallas cried out.

She and Levi rolled to the side.

The man and the bike crashed to the ground in the spot they'd just vacated.

Levi and Dallas didn't have time to process what had happened. More motorcycle engines sounded, echoing off the sides of the bluff.

"We need to get out of here," Levi said.

"What about these guys?" Dallas pointed at the men lying on the ground.

"We can't take them with us. We have to get away before the others find us. We don't know how many more there are." He leaped to his feet and ran for the ATV. "Come on!"

Dallas pulled out her cell phone and snapped a picture of the one lying in front of them. Then she raced to catch up with Levi, jumping on the back of his ATV. As they drove back out into the creek, Dallas held her phone over the man lying in the water and snapped a picture of him as well. As fast as they were going, she doubted it would turn out. But anything might be better than nothing. As long as they lived to tell about it.

Chapter Six

Levi followed the stream half a mile farther, searching for a place where he could climb the bank out of the creek bed. "What have we got back there, Dallas?"

"I don't see anything." She paused. "No, wait… Two…three…four motorcycles."

Levi hit the throttle and raced across an open pasture as fast as he could. He didn't like being out in the open when Dallas was on the back. If anybody shot in their direction, she would be the one to take the bullets. He refused to let that happen on his watch. They had to get enough distance between them and the other motorcycles before they reached the break in the fence. They needed time to get past the come-along he'd strung across there.

Dallas removed one of her arms from around him, turned and fired a shot at the people behind her. They swerved but then continued to follow.

Levi hoped he was heading in the right direction. He was following the compass on the ATV that indicated they were headed south. He didn't know how far to the west he'd gone in the creek bed. Finally, he saw the stand of trees where they'd found the deserted meth cabin, and he knew he was headed in the right direction. He just hoped that the motorcycle gang hadn't left any stragglers at the cabin. He blew past the wooded area and continued on, praying that the distance between them would lengthen rather than shorten. When he arrived at the break in the fence, he didn't have to say anything.

Dallas jumped off, disengaged the come-along, then jumped back on. It took less than five seconds. They were on their way again, moving on to the Rafter T Ranch. He didn't have time to stop and pull his cell phone out of his pocket to call for backup. It didn't matter anyway. He figured there would be no cell phone reception as far out as they were. His best bet was to get back to the ranch, get into his truck and head to town. The sooner he got to the sheriff, the better.

"Holy hell," Dallas said behind him.

"What?" he asked.

"I see smoke rising up from where that cabin was."

Levi muttered a curse. The evidence that was

in that cabin would soon be reduced to ash. By the time the sheriff got there, there would be nothing left. And there'd be nothing left of them if he didn't get them to the truck and get the hell back to Whiskey Gulch before the motorcycle gang caught up with them.

They had lost some ground by stopping at the break in the fence. Shots were fired behind them. Levi zigzagged a little to the left and back to the right, afraid that by doing too much swerving he'd slow them down, giving the motorcycle gang a chance to catch up with them.

Finally, he saw the Rafter T Ranch's barn in the distance. His truck was not the only one parked in front of it. Another truck stood next to his with a man and a woman standing beside it.

As he and Dallas neared, the man reached into his truck and pulled out a rifle. The woman pulled out a second one. The man ran for the gate to the pasture that led into the barnyard, shifted the lever on the gate and pushed it open.

Then the man and the woman rested their rifles on the top rail of the fence and aimed at the motorcycle gang.

Levi and Dallas blasted through. Levi immediately stopped the ATV, and they both jumped off and pulled their weapons free. By the time they joined the couple at the fence, the motorcycle gang had slowed to a stop a few hundred yards from the barn. They fired their weapons, and then raced back in the direction they had come.

With the danger subsided, Levi jerked his phone out of his pocket and checked for reception. He had none. He turned to the couple with the rifles. "Is there a landline nearby? Where can I get to a phone?"

"In the barn." The man led the way inside.

Levi hesitated.

"I'll stand guard," Dallas said. "Go. Report to the sheriff."

Levi followed the man into the barn. He'd entered the tack room, lifted a phone and was already dialing 9-1-1. When he had the dispatcher on the line, he handed the receiver to Levi.

Levi explained the situation and asked that a fire truck be dispatched to the hunting cabin on the land to the north of the Rafter T Ranch. "I don't know where it is. Follow the smoke," he said. "And send an ambulance. There are two men down on that ranch as well. If you meet us at the barn on the Rafter T Ranch, we'll lead you out there."

The dispatcher reassured Levi that the sheriff, an ambulance and the volunteer fire department were on the way.

When Levi hung up the phone, he turned to the man who'd led him into the barn and held out his hand. "Thank you, sir. By the way… I'm Levi." With his other hand, he pulled the star out of his pocket. "I work for the sheriff's department."

"Frank Thatcher," the man said and gripped his hand in a firm handshake. "The woman outside is my wife, Marion. You must be the man the sheriff was telling me about who's here to investigate Harold Sims's death." Thatcher shook his head. "I was sorry to hear about Harold. He was a good man trying to get his life on track." He led the way to the barn door.

They walked outside to join Marion and Dallas.

"Any sign of those bikers?" Levi asked.

Dallas shook her head. "They're long gone, and the smoke's rising. I'm betting that meth shack had something to do with Harold's death."

"Yeah, but what?" Levi asked.

Fifteen minutes later sirens wailed, and emergency vehicles filled the barnyard. The sheriff led the pack in his truck, coming to a stop next to Levi. After parking, he jumped down and hurried over. "Are you two okay?"

Dallas nodded.

Levi shook the sheriff's hand. "Yes, sir."

"Want to tell me what happened? I got an abbreviated version from Dispatch." He looked to Dallas, but Dallas turned to Levi.

Levi gave him a brief rundown of finding the meth house, discovering blood and being chased by the motorcycle riders. "We left two bodies in that creek."

"Then let's get out there before something happens to them," the sheriff said. "Can my truck make it out there?"

Dallas shook her head. "No, you need an ATV."

Mr. Thatcher looked at his wife. "There are several available in the barn."

"We need to hurry," Levi said. "The motorcycle gang must have torched the meth house, and they could be on their way back right now to collect the bodies."

Thatcher led the way into the barn to the far stall where the four-wheelers were lined up, along with a two-seater ATV.

The sheriff mounted one of the four-wheelers. The Thatchers took the two-seater ATV. A sheriff's deputy, who'd arrived behind the sheriff, took one of the other four-wheelers.

Dallas opted to ride with Levi rather than take another vehicle of her own.

They rode out across the pasture and through the break in the fence. Less than fifteen minutes had elapsed since the last time they had passed the burning cabin and the creek bed.

When they rounded the corner of the bluff, the bodies were gone.

Levi cursed.

The sheriff turned to Dallas. "Did you recognize them?"

She shook her head. "No, but maybe I can do better. I shot a picture." She pulled out her cell phone. One photograph was too blurred to make out. But the one she'd taken of the man who'd fallen from the bluff was clear. Though his face was bruised, he would be recognizable by someone who knew him.

"Not anyone I know," the sheriff said. "We'll match it against our criminal database. Let's get on over to that fire."

By the time they reached the cabin in the stand of trees, the flames were reaching high into the sky.

The sheriff shook his head. "I'll put in a call to the fire department but, by the time they get here, there won't be anything left to salvage." The sheriff turned to Dallas. "Send me that image. I'll shoot it to my men at the state crime lab, and I'll have them come out and pick through what's left of this shack. And, by the way…" The sheriff frowned at Dallas.

She nodded. "I know. I'm not supposed to be on this investigation."

"No, you aren't, but I'm glad you were here

to keep Levi from getting his one-way ticket to the city morgue."

Levi nodded. "That's right, Sheriff. If she hadn't been here, that's where I'd be. I would have been outnumbered *and* outgunned."

The sheriff leaned close to Dallas. "You better get back to Whiskey Gulch before the state crime lab gets here."

"Yes, sir." Dallas's brow dipped. "Are you going to be all right out here?"

The sheriff nodded. "I'll be fine. I doubt that the motorcycle gang will be back anytime soon." He waved at the flames. "They've destroyed what little evidence we had. All we can hope for is to get a sample of the dried blood in front of the door."

The sheriff and the deputy stayed to stand guard near the burning hut.

Levi straddled the four-wheeler, and Dallas climbed on behind him.

"Do you want us to stay with you, Sheriff?" Frank Thatcher asked.

The sheriff grinned. "It wouldn't hurt to have a little more backup."

"You've got it," Mr. Thatcher said. He and his wife pulled out their rifles and stood ready.

"Hey, Jones." The sheriff lifted his chin toward the Rafter T Ranch. "When you're back at the barn, let the ambulance know that there's nothing to see here. They can head back to the station."

"Yes, sir." Dallas wrapped her arms around Levi and held on.

Levi liked the feeling of those arms wrapped around him. They were strong, capable and feminine.

Levi headed back to the barn, pulling up in the barnyard next to the ambulance.

Dallas dismounted and spoke with the EMT, letting him know the bodies they'd been sent to collect had disappeared.

After Levi loaded the four-wheeler and stowed the ramps in the back of his truck, they climbed into the cab and drove off the Rafter T Ranch.

Levi glanced over at Dallas. "You didn't fight that very hard."

She frowned. "Fight what?"

"Being dismissed. I would have thought that you would have stayed longer at the burning hut."

"It will be a while before the smoke clears," she said. She held up the phone with the photograph of the biker. "In the meantime, we have a clue. We should follow up on it. And as soon as we have reception, I'll forward this image to the sheriff's office."

Levi grinned and focused on the road ahead.

The woman didn't miss a beat. She was drenched in creek water, could have been shot several times, and she didn't let it slow her down one bit. He really liked the deputy sheriff.

BY THE TIME they reached Whiskey Gulch, it was well past noon. Dallas's stomach rumbled. "We should catch a bite to eat at the diner."

"What? You don't want to go interview motorcycle gangs right away?"

She shook her head. "Not yet. I could use some food. I didn't eat anything for breakfast."

"Sounds good," Levi said. "Let me drop the ATV first."

She nodded and waited for him to park in front of the sheriff's office building. She helped him set the ramps on the back of his truck.

Levi drove the ATV down and headed for the shed behind the building while she closed the gate. Not only was he capable of driving a four-wheeler at high speeds across a bumpy pasture, with a motorcycle gang chasing them and firing at them, but he was a good shot and incredibly attractive in a rugged sort of way.

Her gaze followed him as he drove along the side of the office. It was a good thing that he was only on temporary assignment to the sheriff's department. She could get used to having him around as her partner. They anticipated each other's needs and had each other's backs.

When he emerged from behind the building, he smiled as he approached her. "We should probably go change into dry clothes before we go to the diner." He glanced down at his soaked jeans and shirt and nodded toward hers.

She glanced down at her own clothes, which were beginning to steam in the afternoon heat. "You're probably right."

"My place is closer, but I could take you all the way over to yours, then come back and pick you up."

"No." Dallas shook her head. "Let's stop at your place first. I'll wait in the truck if you want."

"You might as well come in. I have some coffee in my cupboard. You can help yourself while I take a quick shower."

She nodded, curious as to where he lived.

He pulled up in front of a small house a couple of blocks away and switched off the engine. "I'm renting by the month. I didn't know if I would be staying. I'll apologize up front. I don't have much furniture, just what was left when I came home from deployment."

She frowned. "Your ex took the rest?"

He nodded. "And it's just as well. I didn't

need the memories. This way, I got to start over fresh."

"I understand that," Dallas said. "Sometimes, it's easier."

He unlocked the door and led her inside. "You can have the best seat in the house. It's practically the only seat besides the lawn chairs the previous renter left in the shed. My first purchase was a metal bed frame and a mattress and box spring, so I have something to sleep on."

Dallas looked around the empty room. "Wow, she really did clean you out, didn't she?"

Levi shrugged. "I figure my past is what made me who I am today, but my future is an empty slate. I can do anything and be anything I want to be."

"That's a pretty healthy attitude after a divorce."

"I like to think so. It doesn't do any good to dwell on the past, as I learned the other night staring up at the stars. The best thing I can do is lay out a plan and embrace my future. Whether it's working for Trace Travis and the Outriders or something else."

"Like going back to the Deltas?" she asked.

Again, he shrugged. "Maybe."

She turned to face him, studying his face. "You miss your team, don't you?"

"Some of them," he said with a grin. "Then again, a couple of them are here at Whiskey Gulch Ranch."

Dallas frowned. "You mean Trace Travis was a member of your team?"

Levi nodded. "As was Irish. I suspect others from our former Delta team might find their way here eventually."

"That would be nice. It would be like a family reunion."

Levi nodded. "They're my brothers." He tipped his head toward the kitchen. "You'll find a coffee maker, which was my second purchase, and coffee on the counter. I won't be long."

"If you're not going to be long, I'll wait on the coffee. We'll have lunch shortly."

He nodded. "Suit yourself. I don't have a TV, but the backyard is nice if you want to step out on the back porch. The woman who lived in the house before me planted a bunch of flowering shrubs and perennial flowers. It's really nice. You should check it out."

Dallas smiled. "Thank you. I will." She headed for the back porch, while Levi ducked into the only bathroom in the house and closed the door.

When she heard the sound of the shower being turned on, Dallas paused at the back door. She could imagine that on the other side of that door was a naked man, one she hadn't known very long.

After what had happened the night before and that day, she felt a kind of connection to him and an attraction she couldn't deny. Was she finally letting go of the sorrow she'd felt over losing Brian? It had been over two years, after all. She was still young with a full life ahead of her. Like Levi said, she couldn't dwell on the past. She needed to embrace her future. The possibilities could be endless, if only she let them be.

Dallas pushed through the back door out into the yard. It was as pretty as Levi had indicated, the bushes lush and green, with bright yellow lantana growing among them. Birds sang and flitted through the branches of trees. What did they know about the three dead men? Nothing. Nor did they care. Nature went on while man struggled to find his way through the world.

For the next five minutes, Dallas meandered through the yard, sniffing roses, inhaling their fragrance and letting the calm of the garden wash over her. What a contrast to being shot at less than an hour ago.

Footsteps on the back porch alerted her to the fact that Levi had joined her.

"I like that you can actually smell the roses," he commented. "You can rarely smell the ones you can buy in a flower shop."

"I think they bred the scent out of them." Dallas bent once more over a bright red rose and sniffed. She loved the soft scent. When she straightened, she pushed back her shoulders. "Are you ready?"

Levi was pulling a T-shirt over his head and down across his bare chest, covering a broad expanse of delicious muscles.

Dallas's breath caught in her throat as she openly stared at the man.

Once he tugged the hem in place, he captured her gaze with a hint of a smile. "I'm ready."

"Good," she replied. In her head, she thought, *Good, because now I'm not ready.* She had just been thinking about the future and maybe moving past her mourning for Brian. But seeing a bare-chested male in front of her frightened her.

Was she ready to let go of the love she'd had for Brian? Did she know how to be in a relationship with a man after having held her dying fiancé in her arms? Would she always compare the two? Scarier still was, would she feel the passion she hoped she was capable of? Or was she just fooling herself, and she was not an interesting lover after all? She drew in a deep breath, ducked her head and walked up the steps past Levi and into the house. "Let's go. I need to get my shower. Suddenly, I feel like I smell like creek water."

He chuckled and sniffed loudly. "Yes, you do. I'd offer you my shower, but I'm sure you'd like to change into your own clothes."

"You got that right," Dallas said as she pushed through the front door and out onto the porch.

Levi followed and locked the door behind him.

They climbed into the truck and headed to her house on the other end of town.

"Did you ever call the man about fixing those windows?" he asked as they pulled up in front of her house.

She shook her head. "No. I completely forgot."

"If you'll share that phone number, I'll give them a call myself and set up a time and date for them to replace them."

"Thanks. I'd appreciate that." She dug her hand into her back pocket and pulled out the sheet of paper that Mrs. Miller had given her with the number on it. Unfortunately, the ink had gotten wet when she'd rolled in the creek and had smeared, making it illegible. "Well, darn," Dallas said. "Guess I'll have to look it up."

"Don't bother. I'll go talk to your neighbor Ruth. I'm sure she wouldn't mind giving me the number again."

Dallas cocked an eyebrow. "Just be fore-warned—she loves to talk, and she loves gossip. She'll have your complete life story before you've been there fifteen minutes."

"So, what you're telling me is that you're going to take more than fifteen minutes to get a shower?" He held up a hand. "Don't mind me. Take as long as you need."

"You should know better than that. You learn to shower quickly when you're deployed to a place where water is scarce. You're lucky to get a two-minute shower in Afghanistan. I'll be done in five," she said.

"See you in five, then."

Dallas walked up the steps to her house as Levi walked across the street to her neighbor Ruth's. She turned as she reached her doorway to watch as he knocked at the woman's door.

Ruth answered with a smile.

Dallas pushed her key into the lock, a grin tugging the corners of her lips. Levi had made events of the past less-than-twenty-four hours bearable by just being there. She was pretty sure that he was brightening Ruth Miller's day just by being on her front porch.

She pushed open the front door, stepped inside her living room and gasped. Red spray paint was stained like blood across the walls and her furniture. She pulled her gun from the holster and backed away and out the front door.

"Levi!" she called out. "Got a minute?"

She didn't look over her shoulder to see if he'd heard her. Instead, she waited, listening for the sound of his footsteps as he ran across the street to join her on the front porch.

"What's wrong?" he asked.

"I've had a visitor."

He pulled his gun from his shoulder holster, stepped in through the door and swore.

She entered behind him. One by one, they checked the other rooms. Whoever had been in there had been in a hurry, and probably hadn't been gone long. The paint was still wet.

Levi and Dallas headed for the back door that had been forced open, the door frame splintered. Levi stepped through the opening and stood on the back porch, staring out over the field beyond.

In the distance Dallas could hear the rumble of a motorcycle. She stood beside Levi on the back porch, her body trembling. Her home had been invaded and desecrated. When she had been chased by the motorcycles, when they'd been riding the ATV and were shot at, she'd relied on her adrenaline to keep her from losing it.

Now, as she stood on her back porch in the only place that she had ever felt safe, she realized that she wasn't safe anywhere.

Levi gripped her arms. "Hey—" he tipped her chin up "—it's just paint."

She shook her head. "It's more than that," she said. "It's a message that they aren't done with me. I killed one of theirs."

"So did I," he said.

She looked up at him. "Then you'll probably be next. Neither one of us will be safe until we stop them."

He forced a smile. "Then it's a good thing we've got each other's backs." He pulled her into his arms and hugged her.

Slowly, her arms found their way around him, and she leaned her cheek against his chest. That solid wall of muscles made her feel more secure. How would she feel when he wasn't there? She was supposed to be a tough cop who could handle anything, and here she was, shaking in her boots, relying on someone else to make her feel secure.

"Go ahead," he said. "Lean on me. Your personal space has been violated. You're supposed to be concerned. Hell, I'd be concerned if it was my house and they'd invaded it."

She absorbed his heat for a few minutes more.

And then he leaned back, tipping her head up again and forcing her to stare into his eyes. "You know what you need to do, don't you?"

"Yes. No." She frowned. "Maybe? Where are you going with this?"

He chuckled. "We've got to crack this case wide open."

"You're a Delta, not a detective." Still, his humor lifted her spirits.

"I may not be a detective, but I am a quick study. Grab some clothes and get that shower. We have some business to take care of."

She nodded but stood in the circle of his arms for a moment longer. "Thank you for being here," she said. "I'm not sure if I could have handled all this by myself."

He shook his head. "Sure you could. You're a former MP and a current deputy sheriff. You can handle anything. I'm just here as your moral support." He bent and pressed his lips to hers, gave her a quick kiss and then leaned back. "Now, go get your shower." He wrinkled his nose. "You smell."

"Thanks for keeping it real." She smiled as she went into her bedroom, where the red spray paint had been sprayed across her bed and her walls, and even inside her closet. She rifled through the clothes hanging there and found some that weren't damaged. She collected underwear from her dresser and ducked into her bathroom, the only room in the house that didn't have red spray paint. In five minutes, she was out of the shower, dried and had her hair combed and pulled into a slick ponytail. She felt like she could handle anything, now that she was clean.

When she walked out of the bathroom, she found Levi using a paper towel to scrub some of the paint off the wall. All he'd managed to do was smear it. "Just let it dry. I'll paint over it," she said.

He gave a crooked smile. "Good. I'm just making a mess of it." He went to the kitchen, washed the paint off his hands and came out. "You ready for lunch?"

She nodded. "I am. Let's go." She didn't bother locking the front door, as the back door was already damaged. And anyone coming through the front door would be in Ruth Miller's view. Her own personal neighborhood watch. She waved at Ruth and climbed into Levi's truck.

"At least they didn't damage your pickup," he said as he slipped in next to her.

"Probably only because it's parked in front of the house, and they came in through the rear."

Levi glanced toward her. "So, lunch and then we continue our investigation?"

She nodded. "Actually, we're going to do both at the same time."

"What do you mean?"

"One of the waitresses at the diner dates a local motorcycle club member. I have a few questions I want to ask her." Dallas clapped her hands together. "Let's get this investigation rolling."

"As long as you remember you're not supposed to be on this investigation," Levi said with a wink.

"Right." Dallas nodded. "Whatever."

Chapter Seven

"How do you know this waitress dates one of the guys from the motorcycle club?" Levi asked.

Dallas grinned. "She's the granddaughter of one of Ruth's friends."

"I should have guessed." Levi smiled. "Is there anything Ruth doesn't know about?"

"I don't think so."

"Maybe we should bring her along on this investigation."

"That's actually not a bad idea. But after what happened with the shooting earlier, I'd hate to get her involved."

"Good point." Levi parked in front of the diner.

They climbed down from the truck, entered the diner and chose a booth in the far corner.

"What's the waitress's name?" Levi asked.

"I believe it's Jessica, but she goes by Jess."

A young waitress approached their table.

Dallas smiled up at her. "Does Jess work today?"

The girl smacked her gum and scratched her arm where a tattoo of a rose was emblazoned across her skin. "I'm Jess. Who wants to know?"

Knowing she wasn't the one who was supposed to be on the investigation, Dallas turned to Levi. "My friend Levi," she said. Dallas left it to him to question the waitress as she brought up the photograph on her cell phone and slid it underneath the table and into his hand.

"Uh, yes," Levi said. "I did want to talk to you. I understand that you might be dating someone in a motorcycle club."

Jess chewed her gum loudly. "Maybe. It's not a crime, you know."

"Not at all," he said. "It's just that I'm concerned about one of the members of the local motorcycle club. You see, someone sent me this photo. I don't know what to make of it. I think this guy might be in trouble, but I don't know who I should contact. I thought about going to the sheriff, but it could all be one big hoax. You see, I don't want to start something with the sheriff if someone's trying to pull my leg." He pushed the phone across the table toward Jess.

She stared down at it, her eyes narrowing. She leaned toward the phone, her face blanching white. "Is he dead?" She glanced up into Levi's eyes.

"Maybe." He shrugged. "All I have is this photograph. You don't happen to know who that is, do you?"

"Holy crap." She pressed her hand to her mouth, her eyes rounding. "That's Jimmy the Snake." She looked up at Levi. "Do you know who sent this to you?"

"It was an anonymous text," he said. "No caller ID."

"Do you know who Jimmy the Snake is?" Jess asked, her voice squeaking.

Levi shook his head. "No. I'm new in town."

She drew in a deep breath and let it out. "Jimmy the Snake is one of the meanest, baddest, most ruthless members of the Snake Syndicate Motorcycle Club. The only one meaner than him is his brother Johnny. Those two are tight. If that's Jimmy, and he's dead, you can be certain Johnny will be after whoever killed him. He won't stop until that person's dead."

"Do you happen to know where Jimmy might have been last night?" They already knew where Jimmy was that morning.

"Yeah, I saw him at the rally south of Whiskey Gulch, at the Hanging Ape Bar."

"You don't happen to know what time he got there or what time he left, do you?"

"He was there when I got there at nine, and he left a bit before I did at two in the morning." The young woman pushed a hand through her hair. "Holy crap. I need to call someone. That's going to completely blow my boyfriend's mind. Jimmy the Snake is dead. Johnny will be in a rage."

Dallas reached out and touched the young woman's arm. "Jess, are you gonna be all right? The people you're hanging with can be a rough crowd. If they're dealing in drugs, it can get even uglier."

She jerked backward. "Me and my boyfriend, we don't sell drugs. That's stupid. That can get you landed in jail. I don't plan on having my baby behind bars."

Dallas and Levi exchanged glances, and Dallas turned to Jess again. "Jess, seriously, you're pregnant? You need to protect that baby. There's some bad things happening with that motorcycle club."

The young woman took another step backward, wringing her hands. "You don't understand." She dropped her voice to a whisper. "Jimmy and Johnny Snake don't let you join the motorcycle club unless you plan on staying. My boyfriend joined when he was seventeen. He's twenty-one now. Even if he wanted to, he couldn't get out."

"What about moving?" Dallas suggested. "Leave the state—heck, leave the country. You have a baby to consider."

Jess nodded, resting her hand on her tiny bit of a baby bump. "Don't you think I know that? Don't you think I care about this baby?"

"Hey, Jess, order up," the cook called from the kitchen.

"We don't have the money to make that kind of move. We don't even have a car."

"How do you get to work?" Levi asked.

"I either walk, or Dylan gives me a ride on the back of his motorcycle. I've been saving my tip money to buy a car, but it just isn't enough."

"Jess," the cook called.

Jess gave Dallas and Levi a twisted smile. "I gotta go to work. I'll be back in a few minutes to get your order." Jess hurried for the kitchen, pushed through the door and came back out a second later carrying four plates, balanced on her arm. As soon as she delivered the plates to a table, she disappeared for five minutes. When she came back, her face was red and tear streaked. She marched over to Levi and Dallas's table. "I just got off the phone with my boyfriend. You lied to me," she said. "You said you didn't know whether or not Jimmy was dead. He is. And you two killed him."

Dallas started to get up. "Sit, Jess."

"No way. You killed him. You're the deputy that killed Harold Sims. Now you've gone and killed Jimmy the Snake and Lee Brevard."

"Only because they were chasing us and shooting at us. It was them or us. Today, we chose to live. And Harold Sims was injured before he staggered out in front of my vehicle on the highway," Dallas said. "I didn't have time to miss him. I suspect he was pretty badly injured to begin with, and when I hit him, it just sent him the rest of the way."

Jess shook her head, her lip curling in a sneer. "You told me you didn't know what happened to this guy in the picture, Jimmy Snake. You were playing me."

Dallas shook her head. "If I'd told you who we were, and why we're really here, would you have told us anything?"

Jess shook her head. "Hell no. And don't think I'm gonna tell you anything else. As it is, I might have said too much. What I've already told you could have put me, my baby and boyfriend in danger."

"Jess, I'm sorry," Dallas said. "We're just trying to find who might have injured or attempted to kill Harold Sims. We found a cabin out in the woods, a place where they may have been cooking meth. Do you know anything about it?"

Jess lifted her chin. "If I did, I wouldn't tell you."

Another waitress walked over to where Jess stood by Levi and Dallas's table. "Hey, Jess, the customer at table six would like a refill on his coffee. You done here?"

Jess glared at Levi and Dallas. "I'm done here." She stomped away to the other table, snagging the coffee urn on the way.

"I'm Barb. Can I get you something to eat?" the waitress asked with a pointed look.

Dallas's gaze followed Jess, wanting to go after the girl and maybe talk sense into her. She couldn't imagine bringing a baby into a situation as volatile as Jess was facing.

"That girl has a temper," Barb said. "But she has a big heart, and she's usually good at her job and friendly to the customers."

Dallas sighed. "I am worried about Jess. I think she's in over her head."

"Between you, me and the wall, I agree. And I tried to talk sense into her on multiple occasions. Her boyfriend isn't all that bad, but he's in with some bad people."

"You wouldn't happen to know where we could find him, do you?" Levi asked.

"Actually, I've given Jess a ride home once before. She lives with her boyfriend in a trailer park east of town. It's the smallest trailer in the park."

"I know the trailer park," Dallas said.

"Just be careful. Some other members of the motorcycle gang live in that trailer park as well. Do you want some coffee, Deputy?" Barb asked.

Dallas nodded. "I'd love one."

"Yes. Please," Levi said. "Could we get a couple take-out sandwiches and the coffee to go?"

Barb nodded. "Can I recommend the roast beef special?"

"Sounds good to me," Levi said.

Dallas seconded that recommendation.

The waitress left them at their booth and was back ten minutes later with sandwiches in a bag and two cups of coffee in insulated cups. "Now, you two be careful out there. This town's had enough drama in the last few months. We don't need any more."

"You don't think Jess will try to follow us out of here, do you?" Dallas asked.

Barb shook her head. "I'll keep her too busy to leave. Now, you two scoot on out of here."

Dallas shot one last glance toward Jess, her chest tight. All she could think about was the baby the young couple was bringing into the world with very little money, no car and one of them belonging to a motorcycle gang with a psycho for a leader. She shook her head as she left the restaurant and climbed into Levi's truck.

He slid behind the steering wheel. "I guess we're taking this investigation to the trailer park."

"Looks that way. Maybe Jess's boyfriend will be a little more forthcoming with information about the motorcycle gang, the meth house and who might have injured Harold Sims."

Levi drove the mile or so through town and out the east side to a small trailer park set back from the main road in its own little circle.

At one time, long ago, it might have been a nice park, but that had to have been a long time ago. Most of the trailers didn't have skirting, and the wooden steps up into the units were rotted or in need of repair. The paint on many of the homes had long since faded, and window screens had holes or were missing altogether.

Dallas leaned across the console and touched his arm. "Don't enter the trailer park."

He frowned and drove past the entrance. "Why not?"

"It might be better if we go in on foot and circle around from behind. I'd rather we didn't alert the entire motorcycle gang that we're coming. It would be best if we can get Jess's boyfriend alone. If we corner him in the midst of the gang, he might resort to herd mentality out of necessity." She shot him a crooked smile. "Besides, I don't feel like shooting anybody else today."

He took her hand in his and held it tightly. "You did what you had to do. If you hadn't shot Jimmy, he would have shot one or both of us."

She nodded. "I know, but it doesn't make it any easier. Again, I'm supposed to serve and protect, not kill. Whiskey Gulch isn't supposed to be a war zone. We're not in Afghanistan or Iraq."

Levi snorted. "It might as well be a war zone, with people chasing us down and shooting at us."

Dallas nodded her head toward the cemetery they were about to pass. "Pull in here."

He chuckled, slowed quickly and pulled in. "Are you trying to make a point or is it just coincidence?"

"Coincidence," she said. "We can park under that tree and walk through the field to the backside of the trailer park."

He did as she suggested and parked his pickup beneath the tree. They dropped down out of the truck and tromped across a field, heading for the backside of the trailer park. The field was full of tall grass and wildflowers.

"Maybe we should pretend to be a couple enjoying nature's bounty of wildflowers. That way if anybody in the trailer park is watching, they won't suspect that we're coming to visit one of their own."

"Good idea." Levi held out his hand.

Dallas stared down at it, her brow wrinkling. "What's that for?"

Levi shook his head. "For our cover. Take my hand."

When she laid her hand in his, he raised it to his lips and pressed a kiss to the backs of her knuckles. "Don't you think I'd make a good actor?" he said, forcing his tone to remain light when the intensity of his longing threatened to overwhelm him. He wanted to pull her into his arms and press his lips to her lips, not just to her knuckles.

"After we talk to Jess's boyfriend, I'd like to run by the medical examiner's office," Dallas said, her voice a little strained. She pulled back from Levi, her cheeks red. When she tried to remove her hand from his, he held on tight.

They studied the trailers from the backside of the park.

Dallas spotted it first. "There," she said and pointed briefly at the smallest, most ramshackle trailer of all of them. It didn't have skirting and there was junk piled around it, including an old washing machine, a dismantled hulk of a car and several old tires. The siding had been dented and the door was so weathered in the back that it didn't look like it could hold out the rain.

"And they're going to bring a baby home to that?" Dallas shook her head.

Angry voices sounded from the other side of the little trailer.

Dallas's pulse quickened. She pressed a finger to her lips and eased up to the smallest trailer. The closer she got to it, the better she could understand the words that were being yelled.

"You're lying, Dylan," a deep voice said. "You're the one who's been pinching the stash."

"Marcus, I wouldn't do that," another young man said. Dallas assumed it was the accused, Dylan.

The sound of flesh smacking into flesh was followed by a miserable groan. Someone was hitting another person.

Dallas started around the side of the building to stop it. She hadn't gone two steps when a grip on her arm held her back. She glanced over her shoulder at Levi.

He had his hand cupped to his ear and he wiggled his fingers, indicating they should move closer to the source of the argument to listen.

She eased around the rear corner of the house and walked along the side, hugging the shadows all the way.

Levi followed with his gun in his hand. Dallas had her hand on her gun, but left it holstered. She'd be damned if she shot another person that day.

The argument continued.

"It had to be you. You're the youngest one of us, and my buyer said it was a kid who sold it to him," Marcus's voice growled.

"It wasn't me," Dylan said. "I don't sell that stuff. You know that. I don't want anything to do with dealing."

"You're lying," Marcus said. "You've been pinching it all along. Now you've gone too far and took too much."

"Look," Dylan said. "I'm not stupid. I know what happens to people who steal from the Snakes. I want to live to see my thirtieth birthday."

Again, the sound of flesh hitting flesh and another groan.

Dallas winced and fought to keep from running out to stop the beating.

"Look, I haven't been stealing or selling the stuff. If I was, I wouldn't be living in this dump of a trailer, and I'd be driving a car instead of a wreck of a motorcycle. And I would have moved away from this crappy town as fast as I could."

"No one leaves the Snakes alive," another voice warned.

"Admit it, Dylan," the man called Marcus yelled. "You've been pinching from the club for a while now, and if you're not selling it, you've got your friends selling it."

"Yeah," someone else said. "And you let Sims take the fall for you when he just happened to find the factory."

"Where's the rest of it?" Marcus's deep voice demanded. "Tell us where it is, and I might not kill you."

"I told you," Dylan's weakening voice said. "I don't have it. I don't know where it is. I didn't steal it. I never wanted anything to do with selling that stuff. It ruins lives. If you don't end up in jail for selling it, you die a slower death when you're hooked on it. I don't need it or want it. I...did...not...steal it."

"You got one last chance, dude," Marcus said, his tone low and deadly. "Tell us where it is or you're gonna die."

"I can't tell you what I don't know," he pleaded. "Maybe it's somebody else in the organization. Maybe you're the one who took it, and you're trying to cover it up by blaming me."

"You're not turning this around on me," Marcus's deeper voice said. The sound of flesh hitting flesh echoed off the walls of the trailer.

Dylan grunted with each punch and uttered another groan.

"Give me my gun," Marcus said.

One of the other guys said, "What if he's telling the truth?"

"I don't care if he's telling the truth," the deep voice said. "He has to be lying. Liars don't live long in this club."

"Johnny won't like you killing one of our own," the other guy argued.

"Johnny's not here. We're gonna deal with this problem here and now," Marcus growled. "Give me my damn gun."

"Here," one of the other guys said. "Take it."

"Now let him go," Marcus's deep tone ordered.

"Don't do it, Marcus. Johnny won't like it."

"Then Johnny should be out looking for the thief. We have a customer waiting for that stuff. He's already paid half. If he doesn't get it, he'll come after all of us."

"Killing Dylan won't solve your problem, if he's not the one who stole it."

"If it ain't Dylan," Marcus said, "who's getting his friends to sell it?"

"They're not my friends," Dylan said.

"They're your age. You went to high school with 'em."

"That doesn't make them my friends," he said. "My friends wouldn't sell stolen meth."

"Marcus, don't do it. Don't shoot him."

Levi stepped around Dallas and would have gone around the corner, but he stopped when he heard a siren. Gun drawn, he poked his head around the side of the building.

Chapter Eight

Two big guys held the young man he assumed was Dylan dangling from his arms. Marcus had a gun pointed at the young man's forehead. All gazes turned toward the road leading into the trailer park.

"Let him go, Marcus. We gotta get out of here. We don't want to start a war with the cops. We've already lost two of our own because of deputies."

Marcus poked Dylan's head with the barrel of his gun. "Today is your lucky day. You're not gonna die, but if I find out you've been lying, you will. And I won't start with a bullet through your head." He pointed the gun down. "I'll start by blowing your foot away." He shifted the business end of the gun to Dylan's knee. "Then I'll take out your knee. Then your hip. Then I'll take your arm. Then I'll shoot you in the chest. And then I'll shoot you in the head. And you're gonna bleed out really slow."

The two men on either side of him let go, and Dylan sank to the ground. On his knees, he looked up at Marcus. "You're not gonna get that chance because I'm not lying. If somebody within the organization is doing the stealing, and I'm telling you it's not me, you've got a bigger problem."

Marcus kicked Dylan in the gut, turned and strode toward his motorcycle, taking his time despite the sound of the sirens growing louder. He straddled the machine, started the engine, circled around Dylan once, and then took off heading between Dylan's trailer and another, right where Levi and Dallas were hiding.

Levi grabbed Dallas, pushed her beneath the trailer and rolled in behind her. He covered her with his body and waited as the motorcycle gang all blew past them. As the last one darted across the field, Levi rolled out from under the trailer and helped Dallas to her feet. They ran around to the front, where Dylan lay on the ground, clutching his belly.

Dallas squatted beside him. "Are you okay, Dylan?"

"I'm fine," he said between gritted teeth. "Who the hell are you?"

"I'm Deputy Jones," Dallas said. "This is Deputy Warren."

He groaned. "Great. What do you want?"

A sheriff's vehicle pulled into the trailer park and drove to the trailer where Dylan, Dallas and Levi were. When the vehicle came to a stop, the sheriff climbed out shaking his head. "Why am I not surprised to see you two here?"

Dallas remained on her knees beside Dylan. "Sheriff, this man needs an ambulance."

"I don't need an ambulance," Dylan said. "I told you I'm fine. Just leave me alone." The young man looked up. His face was bloody and bruised, his eye already starting to swell shut.

Dallas frowned. "You need to have your injuries checked."

"I'm not going to a doctor." He tried to get up but staggered and fell back to his knees.

"At least let us help you get back into your trailer." Levi hooked the man's arm and helped him to his feet.

"What's going on here?" the sheriff asked.

"From what we heard," Levi said, "the motorcycle club, the Snakes, were hammering one of their own, Dylan here."

Dylan glared at Levi. "You don't know what you're talking about. I fell."

Levi shook his head. "We witnessed a good portion of what happened. Some dude named Marcus had a couple of his guys holding Dylan, beating him up." Levi turned to Dylan. "Is that what all of this is about? Some missing meth?"

Dylan shrugged and winced. "I told you, I don't know what you're talking about."

The sheriff stepped closer. "Dylan, I know your mother. She worked two jobs to get you through high school."

"And she left as soon as I graduated." Dylan spit on the ground.

"She wanted you to go with her," the sheriff said. "She wanted you out of this place. Away from the Snakes. She begged you to go."

Dylan laughed. "People don't leave the Snakes alive."

Sheriff Greer's face hardened. "You mean like Jimmy and Brevard?"

Dylan frowned and winced. "Why? What happened to them?"

"They decided to fire on a couple of my deputies." The sheriff waved toward Dallas. "You've met Deputy Jones, and this is Deputy Warren. Apparently, they found your meth house."

Dylan's brow furrowed. "It's not my meth house. I don't take drugs, and I don't deal them."

"And that's a good thing," Dallas said, "especially since you've got a baby on the way."

He jerked his head toward her, his frown deepening. "What do you know about that?"

"Just that you do." Dallas planted her hands on her hips. "And being a member of a killer motorcycle gang is no way to raise one."

"I tried to get Jess to leave Whiskey Gulch without me, but she won't do it. She has some dumb belief that a baby needs a father. I did just fine without mine."

"And you want your child to grow up without you? Without knowing his or her father?" Dallas asked.

"No, but I don't want her mixed up in this mess, and if it means sending them away, I'll do what I have to do."

"And how can you send them away? You don't even have a car for them to take."

His frown deepened. "I'm working on it. Old Man Campbell gave me a clunker he had sitting up on blocks. As I get money, I'm fixing it. By the time Jess has that baby, it should be done."

"Not if you're dead," Dallas said.

"They wouldn't have killed me," Dylan said. "Johnny wouldn't let that happen."

Dallas crossed her arms over her chest. "Was Johnny there?"

"No," Dylan admitted.

"If they thought you stole their stash of meth, they would kill you in a heartbeat. That's money. A life means nothing to them."

"That doesn't mean they'll let me just up and leave. I know too much."

"Then you need to work on a plan to get the hell out of here." Dallas lifted her chin and stared into Dylan's good eye. "But before you go, we need to know who's been selling that stolen meth."

He shook his head. "I don't know."

"Marcus said they were kids your age doing the selling. Surely you've heard something through the grapevine. Or have some of your old classmates suddenly come into money…maybe riding around in fancy new cars or have expensive clothing or jewelry?"

Dylan's eyes narrowed. "I don't nark on people."

"Yeah, well, there's some bad stuff going down right now, and you're caught right in the middle of it. Your baby needs a father, and Jess needs you alive, not dead," Dallas said. "I understand not wanting to rat on others, but could you at least give us a hint? Maybe tell us if those others doing the selling were in your class? Would I find them in your yearbook?"

He snorted. "My mom couldn't afford a yearbook."

Dallas fought the urge to roll her eyes. She had to get through to Dylan on his level. "No, but I'd bet there's one in the library. What did Marcus mean about letting Harold Sims take the fall for you?"

"I don't know," Dylan said.

"Dylan…" Dallas stepped forward and touched his arm.

Dylan jerked backward.

"You have to think not only for yourself, but for your family. If we can cut the head off the snake, so to speak," she said in a low, intense tone, "you and your family will be that much safer."

He stared straight into Dallas's eyes. "Jess told me what happened with you today and Jimmy the Snake. If anyone should be scared, it should be you. Johnny and Jimmy were tight. Johnny won't forget."

Dallas took another step forward until she was standing toe to toe with the young man. "Then help us put him away."

"Just because you cut off the head of the snake doesn't mean that snake's gonna die. Ever since Jimmy and Johnny's big brother left to work on the oil rigs, things have just gotten worse."

"Is that when they started dealing meth?" Levi asked.

Dylan shifted his gaze to the Delta and nodded. "Judd started the motorcycle club for the joy of riding. It became what it is today after he left. He's not coming back to clean up the mess his brothers made with the group. Judd got married. His wife's family is from Houston, so they settled there."

"Does Judd know what's going on with his old motorcycle club?"

"If he does, I don't think he cares." Dylan's shoulders sank. Suddenly he looked far older than his twenty-one years.

"Dylan, are the other young people part of your motorcycle club, the ones that are selling the meth?"

Dylan shook his head. "No."

"Then what's it hurt you to tell us who they are?" Dallas said. "If we find them first, we might be saving their lives."

He looked at her with a frown. "Why do you care?"

"They're selling drugs to kids and addicts, true, but maybe they just need a wake-up call. They, like you, are somebody's sons or daughters. You're about to have a child of your own. How would you feel if society gave up on him or her because he or she made a mistake?"

"I don't know," he said. "I haven't even had the kid yet. We don't even know if it's a boy or girl."

"Dylan, to your mother, who had to sacrifice a lot for you, you're still her little boy. Don't you think she'd want you to have a second chance if you got mixed up in something like selling drugs?" She was running out of ammunition to get through to the young man.

"If you won't tell us who they are," Levi said, "at least tell us where these guys hang out."

Dylan stared into Levi's face for a long moment, then sighed. "They like to play pool at Sweeney's, and sometimes, you can find them out at the dance hall. Now leave me."

"Not until I help you get into your house." Levi didn't ask again. He looped Dylan's arm over his shoulder and walked him up into the trailer.

Once he had the guy seated in a dilapidated armchair, he cast a quick look around. The trailer had seen better days. In some places, the laminate floor curled, providing a trip hazard to the unaware. There were only two pieces of furniture, one the armchair where Dylan sat. With ripped cushions and a nonfunctioning leg lift, it had seen better days. Next to it was a stained couch that sagged in the middle. There were a few dirty dishes in the sink, but it could have been a lot worse. In one corner of the living room was a pile of parts that appeared to be an unassembled secondhand baby crib.

"When you get ready to assemble that—" Levi nodded to the corner "—give me a call. I have tools in my truck."

"I don't need anybody's help."

"Yeah, well, maybe Jess and the baby do, and it won't cost you anything but a phone call." He found an ink pen on the countertop and wrote down his phone number on an old pizza box.

"Seriously, if you need anything, call me. You don't have to do this alone."

Dylan shook his head. "You don't know the Snakes."

"Yeah, if they're all that bad," Dallas said, her brow furrowing, "they're not friends of yours, and they're a threat to Jess and the baby."

"Don't you think I know that?" Dylan said, raising his voice. "And if they really think I'm the one who took that meth, they'll use Jess to make me talk."

"All the more reason to help us find the people who are dealing that meth. The sooner we do, the sooner we're out of the woods with them."

"I'm not narking," he said. "That will get me killed almost as fast as stealing that meth."

Levi nodded. "I understand, but you have my number if you change your mind. If you don't do it for yourself, do it for Jess and the baby. Think about it." Levi and Dallas left the trailer and joined the sheriff outside.

"How did you know to come out to the trailer park?" Levi asked.

The sheriff nodded to the trailer at the beginning of the park. "There's a Vietnam War veteran living in the first trailer. He calls when he thinks there's going to be trouble. For the most part, the trailer park is usually quiet. The guy who owns it doesn't put up with shenanigans. There's a good chance that he will kick Dylan out after what happened today."

"Just one more thing to add to that young man's pile of troubles," Levi said. "Are we done here?"

"I am, if you two are," the sheriff said.

Dallas sighed. "He wouldn't give us names."

"No." Levi touched her arm. "But Dylan did say the guys that might be selling the drugs hang out at one of the two bars near Whiskey Gulch. I guess that's where we'll be tonight."

Dallas turned to the sheriff. "Do you know anybody who might have some of the yearbooks from Dylan's high school class?"

The sheriff grinned. "Actually, I would know somebody. My wife. She's a teacher at the high school, and she collects the yearbooks from all the years that she's taught out there."

"Perfect." Dallas clapped her hands together. "We'd like to borrow those."

"You've got it." Sheriff Greer tipped his head toward town. "If you want to swing by my place, the wife's making a big pot of spaghetti, and there will be plenty for all of us."

"You don't have to do that," Dallas said. "We've got a couple of sandwiches sitting in Levi's truck we never got to eat for lunch."

"Forget the sandwiches." With a grin, the

sheriff rubbed his belly. "My wife makes her spaghetti sauce and noodles from scratch. You're in for a treat."

"Sounds amazing," Levi said. "We're coming."

"If we're not too much of a bother, it would be nice to have a home-cooked meal," Dallas said. "That'll give us some time to go through those yearbooks."

"And, since you've been here for a while longer than we have," Levi said, "you might be able to point out the young people who've had issues with the law."

Sheriff Greer climbed into his vehicle. "Shouldn't take too long—the town's small. The high school graduating classes is even smaller. Most of the high school graduates leave Whiskey Gulch to go to college or the bigger cities to find work. We can look over the three or four years bracketing Dylan's high school graduation."

"That would be a good place to start," Dallas said. "And the meal will hit the spot."

The sheriff's gaze softened. "Dallas, if you need a safe place to stay tonight, you're welcome to stay at my house."

"That won't be necessary," she said.

The older man shook his head. "You can't stay at your place. I stopped by there earlier. I noticed the two broken windows, and when I went to knock on the door, I found it unlocked. You should have reported this."

"You have enough on your plate right now," Dallas said.

"Well, the offer stands. You're welcome to stay at my house tonight."

"Again," Dallas said, "I don't need to. I can stay at my own."

"The hell you will," Levi said. "If you don't stay with the sheriff, then you're staying at my place."

"I'll get a hotel room," she said.

Both the sheriff and Levi shook their heads simultaneously.

"The point is that you don't need to be staying alone. Johnny Marks might try again to go after you." The sheriff frowned from Dallas to Levi. "For that matter, neither one of you are safe."

Levi squared his shoulders. "Then we'll stay out at the Whiskey Gulch Ranch with Trace Travis and his bunch."

The sheriff's worried expression relaxed. "That makes more sense. More people will have your back."

"Then it's settled," Levi said.

Dallas frowned. "I didn't say I agreed."

The sheriff gave her a stern look. "It's an order."

She lifted her chin. "I'm not on duty, remember?"

Sheriff Greer's lips twisted. "And you're not a part of this investigation, are you?"

Dallas's lips thinned into a straight line. "Fine. I'll stay out at the ranch."

The sheriff grinned. "Mama likes to serve dinner at six o'clock. Be there."

"Thank you, sir," Dallas said, a smile tugging at her mouth. She liked the sheriff. He was a good-hearted man who cared about his town.

"We'll be there," Levi said.

The sheriff started his engine and drove away.

Levi and Dallas walked through the trailer park to the main road and turned toward the cemetery where they'd parked the truck.

Dallas realized she liked having a partner. They looked out for each other and had each other's backs.

"Let's go by our different places during the daylight and pick up the things we'll need to stay out at the ranch," Levi said as he climbed into the vehicle.

She liked him, but she wasn't sure she could be alone in a house with him. A shiver of something she wasn't ready to acknowledge crept through her. "I still think I could stay at my place."

He frowned in her direction. "And disobey a

direct order? Besides, you've got paint all over the place, a broken door frame and two broken windows. You're not staying there."

Her back stiffened. "We're going to need to be at Sweeney's Bar or the dance hall. Probably Sweeney's Bar, since the dance hall's not really hopping until the weekend. And we don't know how long a night it will be. I don't like the idea of driving all the way out to the ranch after that."

"We'll play it by ear," Levi said. "We'll start at your place getting the things you need to stay the night somewhere else. You're not staying at your house."

A stubborn frown dented her forehead.

Levi held up a hand. "There's a time to be stubborn and independent, and there's a time to let others help you. This is one of the times to let others help you."

She huffed out a breath. "Fine." Meaning, not fine, but she'd go along with the plan grudgingly.

Levi drove to her house and entered with her, checking to make sure all was clear before he allowed her to enter her bedroom and collect what she needed.

Dallas stuffed toiletries, shirts, undergarments, shorts and her sneakers into a gym bag, along with an extra set of jeans and some pj's.

When she was finished, she followed him to the front door.

He stepped out onto the porch.

She stood on the threshold looking back into the house. "So much for a fresh start in Whiskey Gulch."

"Dallas," he said, "it's just paint."

She sighed as she pulled the door closed behind her and followed him to his truck. "I know, but it is kind of depressing."

"Just think of it as a chance to change the color of the walls." He smiled. "And I'll help you."

"Just not red," Dallas said with a reluctant grin. She tossed her bag in the back seat of his truck and climbed into the passenger seat and frowned. "You know, I don't like the idea of leaving my truck here. Those goons might come back and decide to do the same to my baby. If you don't mind, I think I'm going to go park it at the sheriff's house."

Levi nodded. "That's not a bad idea."

Dallas slipped out of the passenger seat and climbed into her truck, a little relieved to put some space between her and the former Delta. She was getting too used to having him around and liking it too much. Especially when he touched her. Then her knees turned to jelly, and her heart raced. Truth was, she wasn't ready for anything but friendship.

LEVI FOLLOWED DALLAS to the sheriff's house. His thoughts filled with the woman in the truck ahead of his and how much more he wanted from her than just a partner to solve a case. How had he come to this point with a woman he'd only known a very short time?

Yes, he was attracted to her. She was tough, but easy on the eye and smart. And she knew how to shoot a gun.

He smiled. Since when was being able to fire a gun a requirement for any woman he might consider dating? Still, he found her capabilities sexy, and she made his blood burn.

When they arrived in front of the small house, Dallas pulled into the driveway.

Levi parked in the street against the curb and joined Dallas at the base of the porch steps. He rested his hand at the small of her back, as if it were the most natural thing in the world, and walked up the steps beside her.

The sheriff met them at the front door, still wearing his uniform. "Come in, come in," he said. "Dinner's ready." He held the door for them as they walked inside. The sheriff's home was modest, a single-story ranch of red brick with a wide front porch. The furniture inside was dated, but tasteful and inviting. The scent of garlic and tomato sauce filled the air, making Levi's stomach growl.

A pleasantly plump woman with graying hair stepped out of the kitchen wearing a white apron over a sundress with sandals on her feet. She carried a wooden spoon. "Oh, good, you're here." And she greeted them with a smile. "I'm glad you decided to come. I made too much for just two people." Her lips twisted. "I just can't get used to cooking for two after having had four children to feed."

"Deputy Jones and Deputy Warren, this is my wife, Beverly. Beverly, you know Deputy Jones, and this is Levi Warren. He's working for Trace Travis and his security agency, the Outriders."

"Oh, please, let's not be so formal," Beverly said. "Dallas, it's good to see you again, and, Levi, it's nice to meet you. Please have a seat at the dining table. My husband and I will bring the food in while it's nice and hot. I've set out the yearbooks for the year Dylan graduated and a couple of them on either side of his graduation year. We can look over those after dinner. I might have a few comments I can make about some of those students, because I had them in the class I taught at the high school."

"What did you teach?" Dallas asked.

"English, not everyone's favorite subject," she said with a grimace.

"But necessary," Dallas said.

"Absolutely," she said with a big smile. "So, please have a seat. We'll be right in."

Levi held a chair at the dining table for Dallas. She settled in the seat and waited for him to sit across from her.

The sheriff came in with a big bowl of spaghetti noodles, and his wife brought in another bowl of sauce. After setting the bowls on the table, they returned to the kitchen. This time Sheriff Greer came out with a salad and Beverly carried a platter of French bread.

The table had already been set with plates, silverware and a bottle of red wine.

Beverly sat at one end of the small dining table. "If you don't like red wine, I can get you a glass of water or some sodas if you prefer."

Dallas shook her head. "No, red wine is fine."

"Same," Levi said.

The sheriff took his seat at the other end of the table and poured wine into their goblets.

One by one, they passed the bowls and platters around until each had filled their plate. The dinner was nice. The food was good, and they talked about different people in town, keeping it light and avoiding the discussion of the deaths for that day and the night before. The sheriff had them laughing on several occasions.

Levi enjoyed the meal and the feeling of family. He found his gaze turning to Dallas every time she smiled. She wasn't exactly beautiful, but when she smiled, her face lit the room and made him want to smile along with her. Or kiss her…

When they finished dinner, Levi and Dallas helped carry plates into the kitchen and rinsed them. Beverly loaded the dishwasher, then shooed them all out into the dining room again.

The sheriff collected the yearbooks and laid them out on the table. They started with the yearbook for Dylan's senior year in high school.

"If I recall," Beverly said as she entered the dining room, "Dylan didn't join the motorcycle club until his junior year in high school. His mother was not happy. He worked part-time at the feed store. She couldn't afford to give him a car, and he couldn't afford to buy one, but, when he was sixteen, he was able to purchase a used motorcycle that needed work."

She pointed at Dylan's picture in the yearbook. "He worked hard and was very proud of that motorcycle when he got it running. It wasn't until he joined Judd Marks's motorcycle club that he headed for trouble."

Beverly went on to point out several other

young men who had been challenges in high school. "But most of those boys have gone on to have steady jobs, or their parents got them to go to college or trade school. Dylan couldn't afford to do either, so he went full-time at the feed store. It doesn't pay much, but it's honorable work."

The sheriff gave his two cents' worth. "I know most of these boys from Dylan's class. I watched them grow up. Of the ones Beverly pointed out, some of them left Whiskey Gulch and moved to the big city for more job opportunities. Some went to work on nearby ranches, and others are like Dylan and went to work for some of the local retail stores or businesses."

Beverly pulled out one of the books from the class that graduated when Dylan was a junior. She performed the same assessment of the different boys in the school.

On one page, the sheriff poked his finger at one of the boys in the picture. "That's Evan Billings."

Beverly nodded. "Evan was suspended from school for smoking on campus. He comes from a good family, but he fell in with a bad crowd and let his grades drop. His parents wanted him to apply for colleges, but he refused to go to community college first to get his grades up."

"Since graduating, he's bounced from job to

job," the sheriff said. "There's always something wrong with his boss—they don't treat him right, don't give him the hours or pay he needs—so he moves to the next. I believe he works as a janitor at the dance hall on the weekends. I'm not sure what he's doing during the week."

"Does he still look the same as he did in high school?" Dallas asked.

The sheriff shrugged. "His hair's a little longer and he doesn't dress as sharply, but that's about it."

Levi committed that image to memory. Someone who couldn't keep a job might be easily convinced to sell meth to make money.

"Who were his friends?" Dallas asked.

Beverly flipped the page to another one. "Sean Langley and Nathan Kirk. Usually when you see one of them you see the other two. Sean works at a tire shop, and Nathan bags groceries at the local food mart. They like to get together a lot at Sweeney's for beer after work."

"That's our next stop for the evening," Levi said.

"Do I need to have one of my night-shift guys nearby as backup?" the sheriff asked.

Dallas glanced across at Levi and they both shook their heads. "Sweeney's is pretty close to town. I don't think that anybody would cause trouble. Especially on a weeknight."

The sheriff looked more skeptical. "Normally, I'd say that's true," he said, "but it hasn't been very normal lately."

"We're just going to scout it out tonight," Levi said. "We'll keep a low profile."

"Well, you two be careful," the sheriff said. "It's hard to come by good help in the sheriff's department."

Levi had every intention of keeping Dallas safe. He just hoped she'd go along with his intentions.

Chapter Nine

Dallas tensed as she walked through the door of Sweeney's Bar & Grill. The last time she'd been there, Sweeney had been a jerk. Her gaze went immediately to the bar.

Sweeney wasn't behind it; another man was. She assumed it was Bernie. Levi cupped her elbow and guided her to a table far enough from the bar that Sweeney wouldn't be a problem, but close enough to the door to see everybody coming in and out. While at the sheriff's house, Dallas had used her cell phone to take pictures of the teenagers from the yearbooks. Hopefully they'd find a match with some of the patrons of the bar that night.

Already there were quite a few customers, a mix of ranch hands and townspeople there to let off a little steam after a hard day's work. Their table was between the pool table and the front door.

A man wearing crisply pressed blue jeans

with a starched short-sleeved button-up shirt made his shot, sinking a striped ball into the corner pocket. His next shot was not as fortunate. His opponent, a younger man, wearing a faded black T-shirt with the slogan of a heavy metal band emblazoned across the front and frayed blue jeans, balanced an unlit cigarette between his lips. He leaned over the table and dropped a solid-colored ball in the side pocket. The cue ball kept rolling and tapped another solid into the corner pocket.

As the young man rounded the table for another shot, Dallas got a good look at his face. Her eyes narrowed. "Isn't he…?" She pulled out her cell phone and brought up the photos. She scrolled through the pictures she'd taken from the yearbook and stopped on one. She passed it to Levi. "Is that him?"

The teenager in the picture had neatly combed hair, unlike the unkempt young man standing in front of them. The nose, the eyes, the jawline all matched. The name under the photograph read Evan Billings.

Dallas leaned close to Levi. "He was the one the sheriff's wife said was suspended from school for smoking on campus."

"That doesn't mean he's dealing drugs, but he's worth looking at. Want me to go talk to him?" Levi asked.

"No, let's just watch for now. There might be others that come in."

As if on cue, another young man about the same age as Dylan walked through the door. He stopped, looked around, and when he spotted Billings, he raised a hand in greeting.

Billings gave him a chin lift, then focused on taking a shot. He sank a solid ball in the corner, then tapped the opposite corner with the tip of his cue stick and sank the eight ball there.

Game over.

The man in the nicely ironed jeans slapped a twenty on the edge of the pool table and shook hands with Evan. He returned to his table full of guys dressed a lot like him, sat and took a long swallow of the beer in his mug.

Dallas turned her attention back to the young man who had come through the door. She scrolled through the pictures on her phone, trying to match his sandy-blond hair with one of the photos from the yearbooks. She shook her head, not finding a match to the man's facial features. He didn't look like he could have changed too much in the few years since he'd graduated from high school. It didn't matter. He knew Billings; therefore, he needed to be watched.

Several older gentlemen entered the bar, laughing and talking loudly. They straddled stools at the bar and ordered beer. To anyone watching, it appeared to be just another night after work.

Dallas alternated between keeping an eye on the guys at the pool table and watching who walked through the front door.

A couple of young ranch hands entered in dusty jeans and dirty shirts, and wearing equally dusty cowboy hats. They sat at the table next to Dallas and Levi. Two more ranch hands entered shortly after and joined them.

The waitress brought them all mugs of beer without them ordering.

One of them reached out and patted her fanny. "Thanks, Amy. When am I gonna get that lap dance?"

A young man in droopy jeans had just entered through the front door and witnessed the cowboy's action. His face flushing red, he charged across the floor and shoved the ranch hand so hard he tipped back in his chair and crashed to the floor. "Stay away from my girl," he yelled as he stood over the cowboy.

Amy grabbed his arm. "It's okay, Tyler."

"No, it's not." Tyler glared at the cowboy on the floor. "He needs to apologize to you."

The cowboys at the table leaped to their feet. Two of the ranch hands grabbed Tyler up by his arms and dragged him away from their friend on the ground.

"Let me go." Tyler struggled to free his arms.

Levi started to get up. Dallas laid her hand on his arm and tipped her head toward the man by the pool table. He placed his cue stick in the holder on the wall, turned and walked toward the bar. He entered the hallway to the left of the bar, where the restrooms were located. It was in the direction of the rear exit of the bar. His friend, who'd waved to Evan upon entering, left the bar and followed him.

"I feel the sudden need to visit the ladies' room," Dallas said.

"No, you don't—" Levi pushed to his feet "—but I do."

Dallas touched his arm and smirked. "Please tell me you're not going to the ladies' room."

"Nope. Stay here." Levi worked his way around the group arguing over who should apologize first. As Levi passed, fists started flying.

Dallas left her seat shortly after Levi, giving the barroom fight a wide berth. She headed out the front door and circled the building, heading toward the back. If the two men were going to the bathrooms, Levi would find them there. If they were headed out the back door, Dallas wanted to watch what they were doing or see where they went.

She reached the back corner of the building as a hopped-up sports car pulled away. She ducked into the shadows and waited until it had passed, committing the license plate to memory, although she was pretty sure it belonged to the guy who'd waved at Evan.

Once the vehicle passed, Levi came tearing around the corner, nearly knocking over Dallas.

He grabbed her arms and glared down at her. "What are you doing out here?"

"Getting ready to go tail that vehicle. Let's go." Dallas shook her arms free and took off running.

They raced toward the front of the bar, where Levi had parked his truck. Once they reached it, they jumped in and pulled out onto the road in time to see the taillights of the sports car turn right onto a county highway that headed east of town.

"Hurry." Dallas leaned forward in her seat, adrenaline charging through her veins.

Levi pressed his foot to the floor, pushing hard to catch the car.

Before they turned onto the highway, Levi shut off his headlights, dimmed his interior lights and slowed long enough to allow his vision to adjust to the night. He then slammed on the accelerator to follow the taillights he could see up ahead.

"I hope this isn't a wild-goose chase," Dallas commented.

"Me, too," Levi said.

The sports car picked up speed as the driver left town, until he was moving at over eighty miles an hour.

"That car's built for speed," Levi said. "This truck...not so much." Even with his foot all the way to the floor, they were losing ground as the sports car increased its speed.

Suddenly, brake lights blinked bright red. Levi pressed on the brakes to maintain enough distance to remain inconspicuous.

The sports car turned off the road.

"If I'm not mistaken," Dallas said, "that's the old quarry."

Levi slowed the truck. "What kind of quarry?"

"Gravel," she said. "It's full of water now. Sometimes, the kids come here to skinny-dip. I've been out here several times breaking up parties with underage drinkers."

"Great. So probably selling to minors. We need to catch them. They're probably the ones selling the stolen drugs. I'm going to park out here on the highway," he said as he slowed down before the turn. "How far in is the quarry?"

"Less than half a mile," Dallas said. "Just far enough you can't see it from the road."

"Perfect. We'll go in on foot." He pulled the

truck in behind some bushes, shifted into Park and jumped out.

Dallas met him at the front of the truck.

They moved quickly through the underbrush. Keeping to the shadows, they followed the road into the quarry, trying to be as quiet as they could.

As big a man as Levi was, he was light on his feet and very quiet. He had his weapon drawn and ready, just in case. The starlight peeking through the foliage illuminated their path. When they neared the quarry, they spotted the sports car and one other. Three people stood in the glare of the headlights.

Dallas and Levi knelt in the shadows of a bush near the edge of the quarry, fifty yards from where the men stood. Dallas could hear the murmur of voices but not what they were talking about. There appeared to be an exchange of something between their hands.

"All of my training gives me the urge to run out there and bust them," Dallas whispered. "But I can't. We need to find the source. Who's got the stolen meth? Whoever that is is probably the one who beat up Harold Sims. Right now, we just need to know who those guys are. We can corner them later."

"Agreed," Levi whispered.

All they could do was sit back and wait until

the vehicles left. They knew who Billings was. If they went back to the bar, they could probably find out who had accompanied him. What they didn't know was who was selling to whom and the identity of the third man standing in the headlights.

"We have to follow the other vehicle to learn the identity of the other guy," Dallas murmured.

The three men split up. Evan and his partner climbed into the sports car. The other guy got into the other vehicle. The lone man pulled out first.

No longer blinded by his headlights, Dallas could tell the vehicle was a dark SUV. As it passed, Dallas waited, hoping to catch a glimpse of the license plate. But there was no license plate, and the taillights weren't working. As soon as the vehicle reached the highway, the driver extinguished the headlights as well.

Dallas and Levi ran back the way they'd come to get to their truck before the SUV disappeared. They had no guarantee that Billings would share whom he'd rendezvoused with. If they didn't follow the SUV now, they might never learn who was in it.

As Dallas climbed into the truck, she could see the silhouette of the SUV headed toward town as it vanished over a hill. Levi jumped in and started the engine and shifted into Drive, ready to pull out behind the SUV.

Dallas reached across the console and grabbed his arm. "Take your foot off the brake. Do it now."

He immediately lifted his foot.

A moment later, the sports car left the quarry. As much as Dallas wanted to follow the SUV and discover who was driving it, she didn't want the guys in the sports car to know that they'd been followed, and that Levi and Dallas had witnessed the exchange.

Once again, they fell in behind the sports car and followed it back to town. The SUV had disappeared. Dallas assumed Billings and his partner had headed back in the direction of the bar.

By the time Levi approached Sweeney's parking lot, it was filled with over a dozen motorcycles.

Dallas tensed. "Keep driving."

He glanced her way. "Are you sure you don't want to go in and find out who Billings's buddy was?"

"No way. Not after today." She ducked low as several of the Snake motorcycle club members stepped out into the parking lot to smoke cigarettes. "I don't much feel like another altercation with that group."

"Me either," Levi said. "Are you ready to call it a night?"

"Yes," she said emphatically. "Very much so."

"What about Billings and his partner?"

Dallas shook her head. "I'm not wading into that hornet's nest. We can catch up with him tomorrow. When he's alone."

Levi drove past Sweeney's Bar and farther into Whiskey Gulch, turning on the street to his rental house.

When he parked in front of the cottage, Dallas's heart skipped several beats and then raced. She was about to be alone with a man at night. A man who was practically a stranger and one who made her feel things she hadn't felt…ever. She was nervous. Was she ready? Did she trust him? Hell, did she trust herself?

"Maybe I should go back to my house," she said, refusing to get out of the truck.

He shot a glance in her direction. "No way. For all we know, that motorcycle gang might leave Sweeney's Bar and decide to burn your house to the ground, with you in it. You're not going back to your house."

"I don't want to inconvenience you," she said, realizing how lame that sounded, even to her own ears.

His lips twitched. "If you're worried about being alone with me, I can swear on a stack of Bibles that I won't touch you…" He cocked a brow. "That is, unless you want me to." He smiled. "Seriously, I don't take advantage of women. If you want me to take advantage of you, you'll have to ask." He stepped down from his truck, grabbed her bag out of the back seat and came around to the side of the truck, opening the door for her. "And sleeping in the truck is not an option. So, don't even offer." He tilted his head. "Would it be better if we went ahead and stayed out at the ranch?"

Dallas thought about it for a moment. Deep down, she knew that she could trust Levi to keep his word and not take advantage of her. That really wasn't what she was afraid of. She was more afraid of wanting him to take advantage of her.

Alone with him in his house…

Her mind took off on all the possibilities. None of which she was ready for. Two years without a man in her life was a long time. A flame burned deep inside, threatening to overwhelm her.

Levi held out his hand. "What's it going to be? Stay here or go to the ranch?"

She took a deep breath, trying to calm her racing heart. Then she laid her hand in his. "We'll stay." She slid out of her seat, her foot missed the running board, and she fell into his arms.

He caught her, crushing her to his chest, holding her there until she got her feet beneath her.

Heat burned all the way up her neck into her cheeks. Great, now he'd think she was throwing herself at him.

He set her at arm's length and tipped her chin up. "It really is going to be all right. It's just a night, and we don't have to do anything you don't want to do. I'll even let you have the bed, and I'll sleep in the lounge chair."

She shook her head. "That's not necessary. You're a big guy. You need a decent place to sleep. I can take the lounge chair."

"Actually, the lounge chair is really comfortable," he said as he led her up the steps and into his house. "I slept in it a few nights before I got the bed. Are you hungry?"

"I'm still stuffed from the meal the sheriff and his wife served us."

"Then how about a drink? I have a couple of beers in the refrigerator."

She nodded. "Now, that I could go for."

He closed the front door and strode to the small kitchen. Once he'd retrieved the beers from the refrigerator, he popped the tops and handed one to her. "Why don't we sit on the back porch?"

"Sounds good," she said. "Lead the way." At

least then she wouldn't be alone with him inside the house.

Levi sat on the steps and patted the wood decking beside him. "Sorry, we'd have to bring the chairs from inside out here. I find it easier just to sit on the steps."

She dropped down next to him and sipped her beer. If she'd thought it would be less intimate outside, she'd been wrong. With the stars shining down on them, it was a perfect recipe for making out. She swallowed a big gulp of the beer and settled on mundane conversation. "Do you think you'll get more furniture, eventually?"

He shrugged. "Maybe. I kind of like the idea of owning a piece of land like a small ranch. Nothing as big as the Whiskey Gulch Ranch. But I'd like to have a garden, maybe a couple of cows, try my hand at small-town ranching. I might wait to get furniture until I know what kind of house I'll end up in."

"I thought you were tired of mucking stalls."

"It's really not all that bad. It's good physical labor." He tipped his beer and drank. "What about you? Do you own, or are you renting?" He finished his beer, set the can on the deck beside him and leaned back on both hands.

"I'm on rent-to-buy terms." Dallas sipped her beer, letting the cool liquid trickle down her throat. "I haven't really been here long enough to know what I want."

"Do you think you'll stay?"

Her brow wrinkled. "I'm not sure."

"Why not?"

"In case you missed it, I killed a member of the local motorcycle gang today. It might not be safe for me to live in Whiskey Gulch anymore."

"That makes two of us," Levi said.

"What about you? Do you miss being in Delta Force?"

He nodded. "But like I said before, I have some of my team here. It's like having family close by." He shrugged. "Other than those shooting at me, I like most of the people I've met in Whiskey Gulch. The sheriff and his wife are nice. The women my fellow Deltas have found fit perfectly in our little family. Owning a piece of property appeals to me. I couldn't do that on active duty. Well, I could, but I'd never see it."

"You said you wanted to get on with your life…" Dallas traced her finger around the rim of her beer can. "Does that mean you'll marry again?"

"I don't know. I guess it depends on who I meet. After CeCe dumped me while I was deployed, I'm a little hesitant to commit again. She'd have to be pretty special."

Dallas's pulse kicked up. "Special how?"

"She'd have to be able to shoot straight, for one." He smiled at her. "I need a woman who'll have my back. By the way, thanks."

Dallas stared at her beer can. "You were a Delta for eleven years?"

"Yes, ma'am."

"Does it ever get easier?" she asked.

"Does *what* ever get easier?"

She lowered her voice and whispered, "Killing people."

"For the sake of the mission, you work to improve your skills…and you compartmentalize…" He sighed. "No. It doesn't get any easier. But you do what you have to do."

She continued to stare at her empty beer can. "I had to shoot him."

Levi reached over to cover her hand with his. "It was him or us. You had to do it."

"He was someone's son, brother, maybe even a father."

Levi took the beer can from her fingers and folded her hands into his, turning her to face him on the step. "You had no other choice."

She lifted her chin. "I know. But I can't stop replaying it in my head."

He pulled her closer and wrapped his arm around her shoulders. "Can't you think of something else?"

She shook her head. "Like what?"

"I don't know. Something that makes you happy. For me, it would be riding horses, grilling out with my friends or staring up at the stars with a beautiful woman. What makes you happy?"

She smiled up at him briefly. "Hot fudge sundaes and puppies."

He grinned. "I forgot to add puppies, and I love hot fudge sundaes. Looks like we have two more things in common."

"No whipped cream?"

"Absolutely not. Why ruin a perfectly good sundae with whipped cream?"

Her eyes narrowed. "What about the cherry?"

"Yes!" When she didn't respond one way or the other, his brow furrowed. "No?"

She chuckled and let him off the hook. "Yes."

"Great minds think alike, right?" he said softly, his gaze dropping from her eyes to her mouth.

Dallas licked her lips, suddenly aware of just how close he was holding her and how much she wanted to kiss him.

"I want to kiss you," he whispered.

For a moment, Dallas thought she'd spoken the words out loud. Her lips curled upward on the corners, and she lifted her chin. "One more thing we have in common," she said.

His eyes flared, and he lowered his face toward hers, his hand rising to cup the back of her head. "Tell me no, and I'll stop." His lips hovered over hers.

"I can't," she said and wrapped her arms around his neck, dragging him closer until his mouth touched hers.

Then he crushed her in his arms, claiming her in one fiery kiss that set her blood on fire and awakened the passion that had been simmering beneath the surface since she'd met the man.

She opened to him, thrusting her tongue out to claim his in a long, sensuous caress. After years of being alone, she wanted a man. This man. Not because he was her best friend, but because she found him irresistibly attractive in a very carnal way.

Once the kiss started, she couldn't stop herself. She wanted to get closer. Buck-naked close.

She slid her hand from around his neck to the button on the front of his shirt and pushed it loose.

Dallas didn't stop to think about what she was doing. It had been a day of action. She didn't want to stop and think this one through. She relied on instinct. And her impulse was to have this man, to make love to him and forget about tomorrow.

She had loosened the third button when his

hand came up to cover hers. "Do you know what you're doing?"

She laughed. Then heat flared in her cheeks. "I thought it was obvious."

He tipped her chin up and stared into her eyes. "If we continue this course, I might not be able to stop. My body is on fire with my need for you."

She flicked the next button loose while meeting his gaze head-on. "Yet another thing we have in common. I. Can't. Stop." Another button freed, and she was at the waistband of his jeans. Her hand rested on the metal button. "Do you have protection?"

He nodded. "No regrets in the morning?"

"No regrets," she said. "And no strings. Neither one of us is ready for entanglements."

Chapter Ten

Levi's heart pounded against his ribs. He kissed Dallas hard on the lips and then pushed to his feet.

She blinked up at him. "Are we done?"

He laughed. "Far from it. But my neighbors have a clear view into the backyard. Now, they might be asleep, or they might not. It's up to you." He held out his hand.

Dallas placed her hand in his and let him draw her to her feet.

Then he bent, scooped her up into his arms and carried her across the threshold, kicking the door shut behind them. He turned around.

"Can you manage to lock the door? My hands are otherwise occupied."

She reached out and twisted the dead bolt to the locked position.

Levi spun with her in his arms and strode across the kitchen, aiming for the bedroom with the big new mattress and box springs.

Dallas circled an arm around the back of his neck and held on.

Levi liked the feel of her in his arms. She wasn't so thin her bones dug into him, nor did she weigh him down. Her muscles were sleek, toned and strong. He could imagine her legs wrapped tightly around him. His pace quickened.

Once in the bedroom, he lowered her legs to the floor and rested his hands on her hips. "Still sure this is what you want?"

She met his gaze and raised the ante by pushing his shirt off his shoulders. "I'm sure. No regrets. No strings."

What if I want strings?

The thought popped into Levi's head. He immediately banished it. The ink was barely dry on his divorce decree. Dallas would be a rebound relationship. She was two years past the death of her fiancé. It wouldn't be fair to her if he demanded strings, then walked away.

"No regrets," he repeated. "No strings."

Dallas unbuckled her shoulder holster and dropped it and her gun on the nightstand.

Levi did the same, leaving his gun on the floor beside the bed. Then he gripped the hem of her shirt and dragged it up over her head, tossing it toward the corner.

She reached behind her back and unclipped her bra.

Levi slid the straps over her shoulders and down her arms, dropping it to the floor.

The woman might be strong and tough, but she was shaped like a woman, with breasts a man could cup his hands around.

Levi gripped her hips, reminding himself to go slow when all he wanted was to throw her on the bed and make passionate love to her. Hard and fast.

He wanted her to know he was as aware of her needs as much as his own. Nothing was sexier than a woman crying out in the throes of her release.

His mission was to get her to that point before he slaked his own desire.

Levi cupped the back of her neck and claimed her lips in a slow, sensual kiss.

When she opened to him, he thrust past her teeth to sweep the length of her tongue with his own, loving the taste of her.

Soon, he abandoned her mouth and moved lower, over her chin and down her neck to tongue the pulse at the base of her throat.

Dallas leaned her head back and moaned.

He chuckled and moved lower to flick and lick across her collarbone and downward to the swell of her breasts. When he arrived at one taut nipple, he sucked it into his mouth and pulled on it gently.

Her back arched, she clutched his head and gripped his hair, holding him closer.

He rolled the tip between his teeth and sucked more of her into his mouth.

"Levi," she sighed.

He left that breast and moved to the other, flicking the tip until it formed a tight little bud.

Dallas's fingers convulsed against his scalp, and her breath came in shallow puffs.

He released the button on her jeans, slowly pulled the garment over her hips and thighs, and followed it down the length of her legs until she stepped out of her jeans.

On his way back up, he pressed kisses to the insides of her knees, the sensitive skin of her inner thigh and finally to the tuft of hair covering her sex.

"Want me to stop?" he whispered.

"No," she said, releasing pent-up air from her lungs. "Please, don't."

As he straightened, he cupped the backs of her thighs and lifted her up to sit on the edge of the bed. He parted her knees and moved between her legs.

"You're an amazing woman, all hard as nails to the world, and warm, soft and gorgeous beneath the uniform." Again, he captured her mouth with his and kissed her long and hard, laying her back against the mattress as he did.

His control crumbling, he ran his fingers and lips over her breasts, across her ribs and downward to the tuft of hair covering her sex.

Her body tensed.

He parted her folds, then bent to flick his tongue over her sensitive bud.

Dallas's back arched off the bed.

Fueled by her reaction, he tapped her there with his tongue again.

She tightened her grip on his head. "Levi…"

"Should I stop?"

"Noooo," she moaned.

He took her in his mouth and swirled his tongue over that sensitive spot, attacking it with everything he had.

She writhed beneath him, her hips rocking, her body shaking until she came apart and cried out in her release.

Her body trembled beneath him as she rode the wave to the very end.

Dallas sank back against the mattress, her breathing ragged, and sucked in air. Her fingers still woven in his hair tightened and tugged, drawing him up her body.

He moved over her, dropped his body down between her legs and kissed her mouth. Then he leaned back and drank her in.

Nothing was sexier than a woman who'd come apart with her release. And this woman was staring up at him, her gaze locked with his.

"Don't stop now." She wrapped her legs around his waist and squeezed, bringing him closer until the tip of his shaft nudged her entrance.

The drama of the day, the worry and death faded to the back of his mind, and his heart sang at her words. He couldn't believe they were barely more than strangers. Levi felt he'd known her so much longer. Though they'd insisted on no strings, he wasn't sure he was okay with that. He found himself wanting so much more of this woman.

But not until he had protection. He didn't want a baby tying them together. If they were to develop an attachment, he wanted it to be free of obligation and based on pure love. They needed to get to know each other. This was just the beginning.

DALLAS'S PULSE HAD barely slowed when Levi left the bed.

The former Delta straightened and dug into the back pocket of his jeans for his wallet. He flipped it open, retrieved a small packet and tossed it onto the bed beside Dallas. Then he shucked his boots and jeans and climbed back onto the bed and kissed her again.

She ran her hands over his bare shoulders, across his muscular chest and down his ribs to his waist. His skin was smooth, his muscles hard, and he was gorgeous.

Her hands slipped farther down, cupping his tight buttocks. She wanted him inside her. The sooner the better. Her body still throbbed from her release. Her body craved his. She had to have all of him.

Levi reached for the packet, but Dallas beat him to it.

She tore it open with her teeth and rolled it down over his engorged shaft.

"Now," she said, breathlessly.

He laughed and complied, shifting his body to rest between her legs.

When he touched her there, her heart pounded, her breath became labored, and she couldn't wait another second. She raised her hands to capture his hips and guided him into her with a firm, steady pressure until he filled her.

He remained still for a long moment, allowing her channel to adjust to his length and girth. Then he moved, slowly pulling out.

Impatient now, Dallas tightened her hold on his hips. When he was almost all the way out, she slammed him home again and urged him to a faster pace until he took off on his own, pumping like a sports car's piston.

Dallas let go of his hips and gripped the sheets, raising her hips to meet him, thrust for thrust.

His muscles tensed, his body tightened, his shaft hard and smooth inside her.

Dallas trembled, sensations building to match the intensity of his thrusts. When he slammed into her one last time, an explosion of sensations rippled from her core outward, sending wave upon wave of vibrations to the very tips of her fingers and toes.

Levi remained buried deep inside her, his erection pulsing against her channel. When at last he relaxed, he collapsed on top of her, gathered her into his arms and rolled them to their side and lay there.

"Wow." Dallas inhaled deeply, let the air out of her lungs and pressed a kiss to his chest. "I don't think I could move another muscle in my body right now."

He shifted his hips, his shaft still hard within her. "Are you sure?"

A slow smile spread across her face. "Well, maybe in a minute or two."

He chuckled. "It'll take a few more than that for me."

"Good." She rested a hand on his chest and looked up into his eyes. "I need to recuperate from that workout."

Dallas loved the feel of his skin against hers, her legs entwined with his. It had been so long since she'd had a man in her bed. Making love with Levi had been completely different from making love with her fiancé.

She and Brian had drifted into a tender kind of lovemaking, exploring the difference between friends and lovers, forging a path to a life together at a slow, steady pace.

With Levi, it had been all fire and an explosion of the senses from the moment they'd touched. Would what they'd just shared last? Or, like fire, would it burn out and leave a pile of ashes in its wake?

Why her mind chose to follow that line of thinking, she didn't know. They'd stated up front…no regrets, no strings. Neither one of them was at an emotional state that could handle the confusion and drama of a new relationship.

That didn't mean she couldn't enjoy a man's arms around her and the satisfaction of a good romp on the mattress.

Forcing the negative thoughts from her mind, she concentrated on memorizing every detail of Levi she could, from the way he felt beneath her fingertips to the way he smelled of the outdoors. He truly was a man's man, capable of anything he set his mind to. His ex-wife had to have been completely out of her mind to let this guy go.

They lay in each other's arms for a long time in silence.

The stress of the day eased from Dallas, and her eyes drifted closed. She was almost asleep when Levi's voice rumbled in his chest against her ear.

"About those strings…"

Boom!

An explosion rocked the house.

Her heart pounding, Dallas rolled to her left and dropped off the mattress onto her hands and knees, dragging a sheet with her. She patted the nightstand above her for her gun. When she had it in her hand, she wrapped the sheet around her, crawled to the end of the bed and met Levi coming around from his side, crouched low and naked, carrying his gun.

They maneuvered through the hallway, heading for the front.

The glass from the living room windows lay scattered in shards across the floor.

Dallas moved around the glass and headed for the living room.

A bright glow from outside the cottage lit the interior.

Dallas made her way to the edge of a window and peered around the billowing curtain.

She gasped. "Sweet Jesus."

Levi muttered an angry curse.

There in the driveway, his truck burned like a Roman candle on the Fourth of July.

Chapter Eleven

Levi looked away from the flames and studied the yard surrounding it. Half a dozen motorcycles circled the burning truck and the cottage. The motorcycle riders were armed with rifles and handguns, clearly visible in the light from the fire.

"Stay low," Levi warned Dallas. "I count six bikers, all armed."

"I count seven from my angle. Want me to check the back?"

"No. I want you to stay where I can see you."

"What should we do?" she asked.

"Nothing," Levi said, his jaw tight, his eyes reflecting the flames. "Unless they do something first. How are you on ammo?"

Her gaze never leaving the men on the motorcycles in the front yard, Dallas replied, "Full clip. What about you?"

"Same," he answered.

"Don't shoot unless they shoot first," Dallas said. "We're not in Afghanistan."

"Yes, ma'am." He shot her a quick grin. "Point made. Although, thank you for not following that rule earlier."

Her lips twisted. "Good point. You can shoot if your life depends on it."

"Or yours," he added.

Sirens blared in the distance, getting closer. It wouldn't take long for the sheriff and fire department to arrive. Thankfully, help was on the way.

The motorcycle riders revved their engines and spun their bikes around. Some fired shots into the air. Others aimed at the cottage.

"Duck," Levi yelled and dropped to the floor.

Dallas dived down and lay flat against the floor as more glass shattered.

Engines roared as the gang left the yard, heading in the opposite direction from the oncoming emergency vehicles.

"You ready to vacation out at the ranch?" Levi asked.

Dallas nodded.

He grinned across at her. "You better jump into some clothes before your boss arrives. I'll stand guard."

Dallas glanced down at her sheet-clad form

as if realizing for the first time she wasn't wearing a thing beneath it. "I'll hurry."

She picked her way around the glass on the floor and disappeared into the bedroom. A minute later, she came back out, pulling her jeans up over her hips, wearing her shoes and carrying her shirt and bra. "You're next." She hooked her bra in place and dragged her shirt over her head and down her torso.

Levi hurried to the bedroom, slipped his legs into his jeans and pulled on his boots. He grabbed his shirt and gave a quick glance toward the bed.

The sheets were twisted and both pillows were dented. *No regrets* echoed in his mind.

Only he had a regret. He regretted that they hadn't been able to sleep the night in each other's arms and wake up together in the morning.

He was pulling his shirt over his head when the flashing lights of a sheriff's SUV arrived on the street in front of the cottage. A fire truck, followed by an engine, pulled in behind the sheriff's service vehicle.

"Ready to clear the area for the first responders?" Dallas asked. "I texted the sheriff that we would make certain the area was safe before they got to work putting out the fire."

"I'm ready when you are," Levi responded.

"The front appears clear. Let's go out the back and come back around to the front."

Levi nodded. "No surprises."

"Exactly."

Levi led the way through the house to the kitchen in the back. He opened the door and slipped out onto the porch and down into the shadows of the overgrown bushes.

Dallas exited the cottage, ran down the steps and turned in the opposite direction from Levi.

They moved at the same time, rounding the corners of the house.

Levi didn't like that Dallas was out of his sight, even for a short amount of time. They couldn't be certain all the gang had left the area.

He was almost all the way around to the front when he heard a shot fired. Then another.

His heart thundering in his chest, Levi took off running around the corner of the house and stopped in his tracks when he heard a distinctive rattling.

The sheriff, firefighters and EMTs were climbing out of their vehicles. The sheriff had his gun drawn.

"Stop!" Dallas yelled. "Get back in your vehicles."

"What's going on?" the sheriff asked.

"There's at least a dozen rattlesnakes on the

ground." Dallas stood still, aiming her gun downward.

Levi frowned across at her. "Was that what the shooting was all about?"

"Yes," Dallas responded. "I shot two, but there's a lot more than that out here. Don't let them get under the house."

Levi's gut clenched. He could deal with a dozen Taliban single-handedly, without batting an eyelash. But snakes?

He'd rather not.

Something slithered around his boots.

He glanced down to see a six-foot-long rattlesnake coiling near his right foot, its tail twitching as it shook its rattle.

Levi lifted his hand slowly, aiming the barrel at the head of the snake.

He squeezed the trigger as the snake lifted its head.

The creature collapsed against the earth.

The EMT and firefighters got out shovels and went to work clearing the snakes before they could work the truck fire.

Dallas crossed the yard, shooting the snakes she ran into. She came to a stop beside Levi. "I don't think any of them made it under the porch."

"Thank goodness," Levi said. "Otherwise, we'd have to burn the house down."

Dallas grinned. "I take it you're not a fan of snakes?"

He shook his head. "No. Not at all."

She laughed. "Never had a pet snake?"

"Are you kidding?" He shook his head again. "Who in his right mind would want a snake inside his house?"

Her grin broadened. "Lots of people."

He raised his eyebrows. "Even you? Because if you say yes, we're done. I could put up with puppies in the bed, or maybe even a cat, but I draw the line at snakes."

"No. I've never had a pet snake. But they're not all poisonous or bad." A dent formed in her brow. "You do realize they're not very tall, right?"

"What are you talking about?" His eyes widened. "The one I shot had to be six feet long."

"Long, yes," she said, "but how tall? Maybe an inch at most?"

He frowned. "Okay, you made your point. I don't have to like it. And I don't have to like snakes."

Sheriff Greer joined them. "What happened here?"

"Snakes," Levi said at the same time as Dallas.

"I know there were snakes, but is that why you set your truck on fire?"

Levi shook his head. "The motorcycle gang, the Snakes, did this."

"You know that for sure?" the sheriff asked.

"If it wasn't them, it was another motorcycle club. They watched it burn for a while until the sirens scared them off," Dallas said.

The sheriff shook his head. "I'm betting Johnny Snake is behind this. And I'll also wager it will get worse before it gets better."

"Especially if they're not having any luck finding who stole the stash of methamphetamine." Dallas pressed her lips together. "I don't like being targeted. This has to end soon, one way or another."

The sheriff's eyes narrowed as he glanced from Dallas to Levi and back to Dallas. "I thought you two were going to head out to the Whiskey Gulch Ranch for the night."

Dallas blushed. "I talked Levi into staying the night at his place instead of going all the way out to the ranch." She grimaced. "I'm afraid my mistake has cost him his truck."

Levi shrugged. "It's just a truck."

"At least neither one of you was hurt." Sheriff Greer sighed. "Other than the fact you killed Johnny's brother, if the Snakes are having troubles finding their missing stash, they might think you two took it off Sims and are hiding it from everyone else instead of turning it over as evidence."

"That would be unfortunate. I'm not in the habit of committing crimes," Dallas said. "I'm an officer of the law. I help to enforce them, not break them."

"They might be getting desperate," the sheriff insisted. "If they're supposed to deliver it to their buyer soon, they have a huge problem. You can't deliver what you don't have."

Dallas crossed her arms over her chest and lifted her chin. "Guess they'll continue to suffer. We can only hope the drugs have been destroyed so that they don't get into the hands of innocent children or less-than-innocent teens. By the way, what have you heard from the medical examiner about Harold Sims?"

The sheriff's lips pressed into a thin line. "It's like you said. He sustained injuries prior to you running into him. Blunt force trauma to the skull multiple times. It's a miracle he was able to stumble onto the highway at all. More than likely, whoever did it left him for dead. He probably would have died due to bleeding on the brain if you hadn't put him out of his misery first."

Dallas's stomach churned. It didn't help, knowing she wasn't the one who'd put him in the grave. The man had to have gone through hell. Then to rise from practically dead...

Levi slipped an arm around her waist and pulled her against him. "You didn't kill him."

"No," she said, her jaw hardening. "But some-one did. That someone needs to pay for doing that. Harold was a nice man. He never hurt any-one."

"We'll find the guy," Sheriff Greer said.

"We did a little sleuthing of our own tonight," Levi admitted.

"Oh, yeah?" The sheriff cocked an eyebrow. "What did you find?"

"Not a whole lot, but since we figured the missing stash of meth could be at the bottom of what's going on, we hung out at Sweeney's Bar like we said we were going to do."

"What did you discover?" The sheriff shook his head. "Or should I say who did you dis-cover?"

"We waited for some of the guys you and your lovely wife had mentioned as behaviorally challenged," Dallas said. "We found a winner, we think."

The sheriff's brow rose. "Who?"

"Evan Billings was playing pool when we got there."

"So?" The sheriff stared from Dallas to Levi. "How does that make him a suspect for selling the stolen meth?"

"He left the bar with a buddy of his driving a souped-up sports car."

"Would it have been a black Camaro with the rear end jacked up?" Sheriff Greer asked.

Dallas nodded. "That's the one."

The sheriff nodded. "Sean Langley. He works at the tire shop in town. He and Billings hang out on occasion at Sweeney's. Again, that doesn't make him a suspect."

"A fight broke out in the bar. While everyone's attention was on the scuffle, Billings and Langley left in the sports car," Levi said.

The older man frowned. "So?"

Dallas continued. "We followed them out to the quarry east of town, where they met up with someone in a dark SUV. We didn't see what they were exchanging, but something passed between their hands."

"Who was in the dark SUV?"

"We didn't see his face and couldn't follow him because the SUV left first. Billings and Langley got in front of us and kept us from following the SUV to its destination."

"Are you sure you didn't see what they were exchanging?" Sheriff Greer asked.

"No, sir," Levi said. "We were too far away, and their hands were shadowed."

"It's a start. If they're selling meth, they have

to have a source." Sheriff Greer nodded. "I can see about questioning Billings and Langley."

"They went back to Sweeney's after their rendezvous in the quarry," Dallas said. "I don't know if they're still there."

"I'll check. If they aren't, I'll catch them at work tomorrow." The sheriff glanced at the firefighters dousing the remaining puffs of smoke from the vehicular fire. "In the meantime, let the guys put out the rest of this fire. I'll give you a ride to the Whiskey Gulch Ranch."

"If it's all the same to you, Sheriff," Dallas said, "you can just give us a ride to your house. We can take my truck."

The sheriff frowned. "You sure it'll get you there?"

Dallas sighed. "You men have so little faith in my truck. I'm telling you, it's a classic, and it hasn't failed me yet."

"Key word being *yet*." The sheriff smiled. "Sure. I can give you a lift to my house."

"Let us grab what we can from the house, and we'll go with you to get Dallas's truck," Levi said. "I imagine her truck will run better than mine in its current condition."

The three of them glanced toward the smoking hulk of what was left of Levi's beautiful truck and shook their heads in unison.

Dallas almost laughed at her own grief over

a truck. But then, she knew how she'd feel if someone destroyed her beloved antique. It wasn't just a truck. It was a link to her past, her fiancé and a life she wouldn't have with him.

Levi held out his hand.

She took it, and they walked back into his cottage and grabbed the bags they'd packed in case they did end up at the ranch. It was too easy. Like this had been the answer all along. If only Dallas hadn't talked Levi into staying in town...

LEVI HELD THE door for Dallas as she left the cottage. He was unhappy about the loss of his truck, but it was just a mode of transportation. Though it would be a pain to find another, it could be done. The sooner the better. He didn't like being without wheels.

Dallas climbed into the back seat of the sheriff's vehicle, her gaze on the broken window.

"Do you want me to board it?" Levi asked.

She shook her head. "No. It doesn't matter, and I don't want to waste time."

Levi hesitated beside the door. "You can sit up front. I'll sit back here."

"No," she said. "I'm supposed to be the one on administrative leave."

"Sadly, that's true. And you don't follow orders very well." Sheriff Greer slipped into the driver's seat. "The ME's report clears you completely of Sims's death, but then there's the matter of the Jimmy Marks shooting."

Dallas nodded. "All the more reason to let Levi continue this investigation."

"With my backup," Levi added. "I wouldn't be alive today without her."

"I shouldn't encourage you, Jones, but I need you on this case." The sheriff gave her a stern look. "As long as it stays off the record. I could lose my job, and the entire department could be put under investigation, if the state finds out you're still on the case."

"You can always say you deputized me to protect her. She has been targeted by the motorcycle club."

"That's going to be my story, and I'll stick to it." The sheriff shifted into gear and drove to his house.

Levi texted Trace Travis to let him know that they'd be headed his way within the next hour. Dallas would need a room, but he could sleep on a couch or lounge chair.

Will fill you in on what's going on in the morning.

Trace responded. We have rooms for both of you. Come on out. Will leave the door unlocked.

Warmth filled Levi's chest. He knew he could count on Trace, Irish or any one of the members of his old Delta team. They were there for him as much as he was there for them.

Dallas's truck stood where they'd left it in the driveway, old and intact, unlike Levi's newer-model, now-fried pickup.

As Dallas approached the vehicle, she ran her hand over the side of the truck bed as if touching an old friend.

Levi's groin tightened as he recalled how it had felt to have her hands roaming over his body less than an hour ago.

She glanced back at him, her eyelids at half-mast, her lips still swollen from being kissed so thoroughly.

Damn the motorcycle club for interrupting something that had been so amazing it had given him hope for his future. Maybe he wasn't done with relationships after all.

That nagging question at the back of his mind reared its ugly head.

What if Dallas was a rebound?

Dallas climbed up into the seat of her ancient pickup and glanced his way.

Her sandy-blond hair was still tangled from their tumble in the bed. If anything, it made her even more beautiful and just a little vulnerable.

After all that had happened, he wondered if he'd taken advantage of that vulnerability.

A grin slipped up the sides of his face. She'd

been the one to initiate, not him. His smile slipped. Maybe he shouldn't have taken her up on her offer of sex without strings.

All these thoughts winged through his head as he watched her through the windshield of her old pickup. The truck seemed as much a part of her as the jeans she wore. She didn't wear makeup and didn't need it. Dallas had a natural, unaffected beauty that glowed from the inside.

Levi climbed into the passenger seat. The leather seats were worn, but not cracked or torn. Though the paint on the old truck had seen better days, someone had taken care of the inside. The steering wheel was worn from many years of hands gripping it.

Dallas's slender fingers gripped the wheel now as she started the engine with a twist of the key.

Sheriff Greer leaned into Dallas's open window. "If you two need help or backup, call. Don't try to handle everything on your own."

"Yes, sir," she said. "Same goes for you. Let us know where you get with Evan and Sean. If you don't find them tonight, we'll catch up with them tomorrow and see what we can get out of them. And don't stay up all night. You can't work twenty-four seven."

"What are you? My mother?" The sheriff smiled, the lines on his face appearing deeper than normal. "I don't plan on staying up past midnight. I have someone covering your shift."

"I'm sorry. I'd pull it if…"

The sheriff waved her comment away. "I know you would. It's protocol. We have to follow it." He stepped away from the vehicle. "Get some rest."

She nodded, shifted into Reverse, backed out of the driveway and drove away from the sheriff's house.

"Do you know the way out to the ranch?" Levi asked.

She nodded. "I've been out there once before. It's not hard to find."

Levi relaxed against the seat with the window down and the warm Texas air blowing through at sixty miles an hour as they left the town of Whiskey Gulch.

The wind noise gave them an excuse not to talk as Dallas drove out to the ranch.

She slowed as she neared the turnoff and eased over the cattle guard at the gate.

The long gravel drive wound between trees and opened to the sprawling ranch house with the wraparound porch.

The outside light burned over the front door, and a light shone from the living room window.

As Dallas parked in front of the house, Trace stepped out onto the porch, followed by his mother. Rosalynn wore a bathrobe. Trace had on jeans and a T-shirt and was barefoot. Lily, Trace's fiancée, wore a long T-shirt that probably belonged to Trace and a pair of faded jeans. She was barefoot as well.

Levi climbed down from Dallas's truck and met Dallas as she rounded the front of the vehicle.

He took her hand and led her up the steps to where the three people stood.

The older woman, Trace Travis's mother, opened the door. "Come in. You two must be tired and hungry."

"Not hungry," Dallas said, "but I could stand a drink of water."

"Could I get you something stronger?" Trace Travis asked. "I understand you two have had a helluva couple of days."

"You heard?" Levi met Trace's gaze.

His boss and friend nodded. "About Harold Sims and Jimmy Marks and Lee Brevard. Is there more?"

Levi nodded. "It only gets better. But don't let us keep everyone up. It's late."

"Mom and Lily can show Deputy Jones to her room, while you and I have a beer," Trace said.

"I'd rather have a beer with you," Dallas said. "But I don't want to keep anyone awake."

Lily and Rosalynn looked at each other.

"We've been up since before dawn with a sick calf. Otherwise, we'd join you. But we'll be up again at dawn to check on the calf and its mama."

"Please, don't stay up on our account," Dallas said.

"Trace can show you to the rooms," Rosalynn said.

"There are fresh sheets and towels laid out for your use," Lily said. "If you need anything, don't be afraid to ask. We'll see you in the morning. Hope you like eggs and bacon. That's what we're fixing for breakfast."

"You don't have to cook for us," Levi said. "We can get something in town. We just needed a safe place to stay tonight."

"You should be safe here," Trace said. "Come into the kitchen. I'll get you those beers, and you can tell me what's happened."

Trace led the way into the kitchen, fished three longneck bottles of beer from the refrigerator, twisted the tops off and handed one each to Levi and Dallas.

"Tell me about it," he invited.

Levi turned to Dallas. "You want to start?"

She sighed and launched into the beginning event that kicked off the investigation.

Levi picked up where he'd come across Dallas at the scene of the accident and how they'd gone out to the Rafter T Ranch and followed the cows through the fence to the meth house. Then he continued with the story, relating how they'd been chased by the motorcycle gang and had to shoot the two Trace had mentioned.

"Then there was the paint all over the inside of Dallas's house, tailing Evan Billings and having my truck destroyed by the Snakes," Levi wrapped up in a digest version of what had occurred that evening alone.

"Wait… What happened to your truck?"

"Boom." Levi shook his head. "The Snakes lit it up. Thankfully, we parked Dallas's truck at the sheriff's house for safekeeping, or I'd have had to find another way to get out here. Because we couldn't stay in town."

"That's obvious," Trace said. "You'll stay here indefinitely."

Levi nodded. "At least until the Snakes can be stopped."

"Good luck with that," Trace said. "They've been running wild for a while, from what I've heard through the grapevine. It's a shame. It started out as a club for people who enjoyed riding. Judd Marks was my classmate. He grew up on the wrong side of the tracks, but he never caused any trouble. And he's gone on to work for an offshore oil rig. Made good for himself."

"Yeah, well, his brothers have gotten the gang messed up with drugs," Levi said. "They're making and dealing meth."

Trace shook his head. "That's a shame. Meth is some rough stuff, from what I've read."

Dallas nodded. "And someone's stolen their supply, and they want it back."

"And they want revenge for the deaths of Jimmy Marks and Lee Brevard."

"Which places you two between a rock and a hard place, I take it," Trace said with a twisted smile.

Levi nodded. "We need to find who left Harold Sims to die and who stole the stash and is dealing it in the county."

"I believe you have your work cut out for you," Trace said. "We can talk to the rest of the team in the morning and see if they have anything to add."

Levi tipped his bottle back and drank the last swallows of his beer.

Dallas smacked her empty bottle on the table. "Thank you for the beer. I could use a shower and a bed. We have a lot of ground to cover tomorrow."

Levi nodded, gathered their empty bottles, then rose from the table to find a trash receptacle to drop them into.

"Under the sink," Trace said.

Dallas beat him there and opened the cabinet door for him.

He dropped the bottles into the recycle bin and straightened.

"I'll show you two to your rooms. You've got to be tired after such an eventful day." Trace led the way out of the kitchen and up a staircase to the second floor.

He paused at the door to the second room on the landing. It stood open to show a quaint room with a white iron bed covered in a patchwork quilt. He turned to Dallas. "Mom thought you might like this room."

"It's great," she said and tossed her bag onto the floor.

"The next one is yours." Travis led Levi to the room beside Dallas's. "The bathroom is across the hall. If you need anything, Lily and I are at the end of the hallway. Don't hesitate to knock on the door."

"We should be fine," Levi assured him. "Thank you." He stepped into his room and admired the more masculine decor, with the four-poster bed covered in a navy-blue-and-brown comforter. A small leather sofa faced a window.

He'd left the door open on purpose, listening to the sound of Trace's footsteps. As soon as the door closed at the end of the hall, Levi leaned out of his doorway.

Dallas leaned out at the same time.

He grinned. "Are you showering first?"

She nodded. "Unless you want to go first."

"No. Go ahead."

She clutched her toiletries kit and clothes to her chest and scurried past him to the bathroom.

When she reached it, she turned, looked in both directions down the corridor and then crooked her finger at him.

He frowned and poked his thumb at his chest and mouthed, "Me?"

She nodded and tipped her head toward the bathroom behind her.

Levi didn't need to be told twice. He flew down the hall, captured her in his arms and crushed her lips with his, walking her backward into the bathroom and closing the door behind them with a soft click.

That night ended on a positive note, with him making love with her in the shower and then in his bedroom on the couch and then in her bedroom on the white iron bed.

No regrets.

Chapter Twelve

The morning dawned with sunlight edging around the blinds in the room.

Dallas blinked her eyes open. The unfamiliarity of her surroundings confused her for a moment until she remembered she'd stayed at the Whiskey Gulch Ranch. The events of the past couple of days flooded into her memory, culminating with the bright spot of last night.

She was deliciously sore between her thighs, the ache reminding her of what she'd done and with whom.

Dallas stretched, expecting her hand to touch Levi's broad, muscular chest. When it encountered a soft empty spot on the mattress, she turned onto her side with a frown.

Where had Levi gone? And why so early?

She rolled over to where she'd left her phone on the nightstand and brought up her clock. It was already seven in the morning. Probably past the time Levi got up. Didn't he say he usually mucked stalls in the morning?

Shouldn't she help since she was staying at the ranch?

Dallas kicked off the sheet and rolled out of the bed, standing naked in the dim light making its way around the edges of the closed blinds.

She hooked her bra in place, tossed a shirt over her head and dressed in jeans and her boots. She ran a brush through her long blond hair and thought for the thousandth time she should cut it short so that it wasn't in the way. For the moment, she pulled it back in a low braid at the base of her neck and hurried across to the bathroom, where she brushed her teeth and examined her face in the mirror.

Her cheek and neck were slightly red where Levi's five-o'clock shadow had rubbed against her skin. She smiled at herself.

No regrets.

Her smile faded.

No strings.

She'd promised him no strings. However, after last night, the thought of a one-night stand didn't seem nearly enough.

With a sigh, she left the bathroom, tossed her toothbrush in her toiletries kit and headed downstairs, inhaling the scent of bacon and toast.

Dallas's stomach rumbled. She followed the heavenly smells and sounds to the kitchen.

"There you are." Lily Davidson smiled as she carried a platter of eggs to the large kitchen table. "I hope you're hungry. We made enough food to feed an army. Irish, Matt, Aubrey and Tessa will be joining us for breakfast. With the rest of us, that'll be nine." She stared at the eggs, her brow furrowing. "I hope that's enough." Then she looked up and smiled again. "Did you sleep well?"

Heat filled Dallas's cheeks as she lied, "Yes, I did. Thank you." It wasn't a complete lie. What little sleep she'd gotten had been deep and restful. There just hadn't been much of it after making love into the wee hours of the morning.

"The guys are out taking care of the animals. They should be coming in at any minute." Rosalynn Travis carried a platter of bacon and sausage to the table. "What would you like to drink with your breakfast? Coffee, orange juice or milk?"

"I could use a large cup of strong coffee," Dallas said. "But I can get it myself."

"Strong is the only way we have it around here." Mrs. Travis tipped her head toward the counter where the coffee maker stood with a carafe full of rich, steaming coffee. "Help yourself. There are mugs in the cabinet above the coffee maker."

Dallas found the mugs, filled one and was lifting it to her lips when heavy footsteps sounded on the back porch.

Trace Travis opened the door and stood to the side to allow the pretty red-haired and green-eyed home health-care nurse, Aubrey Blanchard, through. Dallas knew her as Matt Hennessey's woman.

Aubrey turned and looked over her shoulder as she laughed and said, "You should have seen the look on Matt's face when that bull charged him. I've never seen a man move faster."

Male and female laughter sounded out on the porch.

Aubrey crossed the threshold smiling. When she spotted Dallas, her smile broadened. "Good morning, Deputy Jones."

"Good morning, Ms. Blanchard," Dallas said. "Please, call me Dallas."

"And you must call me Aubrey." She winked. "No formalities around here."

She was followed by the pretty strawberry blonde, Tessa Bolton, Joseph "Irish" Monahan's fiancée. Dallas had run into her at the hospital on several occasions. Tessa nodded toward Dallas. "Sorry to hear about your house. Irish and

I can come help you when you're ready to paint over the damage."

"Thank you," Dallas said.

Matt Hennessey entered, shoving a hand through his black hair that always seemed in need of a good cut. His dark gaze found Aubrey, and he moved to stand beside her, his hand resting at the small of her back. "You can count us in as well," he said.

"Supply the beer, and we'll all be there," Lily said with a laugh. She laid a plate stacked high with toast in the middle of the table. "Wash your hands," she said to the men coming through the door. "Breakfast is ready."

The group moved through the kitchen to the bathroom in the hall.

Trace blocked Lily on her way back to the kitchen sink and pressed a kiss to her lips.

She smiled up at him and swatted his arm. "Go on. You need to wash up, too."

"I couldn't resist a taste of my honey, first," he said with a smile. When he tried for another kiss, she swatted him again. "I'm going." He chuckled on his way to the line in the hallway.

One by one, the men and women filed into the kitchen and poured their drinks of choice. Once they had everything, they gathered around the table, waiting for the matriarch, Rosalynn Travis, to take her seat.

Trace held her chair.

"Please, don't wait on me," Rosalynn said as she lowered herself into the chair and scooted forward.

As they sat around the table, everyone started talking at once. Dallas sat with Lily on one side and Levi on the other. Food platters passed from hand to hand until everyone had a plate full of eggs, bacon, sausage and toast.

Trace lifted his mug full of coffee. "To the cooks. Thank you for keeping our bellies full and our hearts even fuller."

"To the cooks!" chimed all around the table. Everyone grew quiet as they dug into the fluffy scrambled eggs.

Irish slathered jelly onto a piece of toast, then shot a glance across the table at Levi. "I hear your truck took a hit last night."

Levi nodded. "Motorcycle gang decided to torch it."

Irish shook his head slowly and he laid his knife on his plate. "Things are getting out of hand in Whiskey Gulch. What is the sheriff doing about it?"

"I'm betting he's canvassed the neighborhood for eyewitnesses," Dallas said. "The department is so shorthanded, I don't see how they can keep up."

Matt passed the plate of bacon and sausage

to his left. "I thought that's why they deputized Levi."

"Still, it's not enough," Dallas said. "We were understaffed even before I was put on administrative leave."

"It all seems so Wild West," Aubrey said. "Only the gang isn't riding in on horseback to terrorize the town."

"No." Trace frowned. "They're riding in on motorcycles, shooting at houses and burning trucks. What can the rest of our Outriders do to help?"

Levi's jaw hardened. He reached beneath the table to grip Dallas's hand. "Be ready in case we need backup. I don't know what they're going to do next. I feel like we're getting closer to the truth about who killed Harold Sims and who stole the missing meth. I'm sure it's going to get hotter in Whiskey Gulch when we narrow in on the killer."

Dallas squeezed his hand beneath the table and nodded. "We've been shot at and would be dead now, if Jimmy the Snake had had his way."

"All you have to do is call." Trace glanced around the table at the members of his team. "We'll be there."

Irish gave Levi a chin lift. "We take care of our own."

Matt set his fork on his plate and lifted his coffee. "Damn right we do."

"Which reminds me..." Trace leaned back in his chair. "I got word from Becker Jackson yesterday. He's separating from the army this week."

Irish and Levi leaned forward.

"He's coming to us, isn't he?" Levi asked.

Trace nodded with a grin. "He is. Should be here by the end of the week."

Irish and Levi clapped their hands.

"Word is getting out about our capabilities," Trace continued. "I have a couple of leads on potential clients. It won't be long before we're inundated with requests to provide protection and security services to more people than we have agents to manage."

"Sounds like the sheriff's department," Dallas noted. "While you're recruiting for the Outriders, please put in a good word for the county sheriff's force. It's not a bad place to work. Pay's not great, but the work can be rewarding."

Trace nodded. "I'll do that. Our old Delta Force team is experiencing turnover. It's probably time for more of them to step down and let the younger men take the lead."

Irish laughed. "You make them sound old."

Levi shook his head. "They're no older than we are. Being a Delta is best left to the young men, but I don't consider myself old. Not at thirty-three."

"Far from it," Dallas agreed.

"Right. You're not old until you're thirty-four…right?" Aubrey winked at Matt.

"Hey, watch it." Matt leaned over and kissed Aubrey's lips. "You're not far behind me."

"Age is just a number," Trace said. "It's where you want to be in life that should influence your choices." He reached for Lily's hand. "I could have gone back into the army and back to the Deltas."

Lily nodded. "I'd have gone with you."

He gave her a brief smile. "I need to be here to manage the family ranch. It's my legacy, and I'm not willing to let it slip out of the family without a fight. That's why I'm here." He raised Lily's hand to his lips and pressed a kiss to the backs of her knuckles. "Best decision I ever made."

She smiled into his eyes.

Dallas's heart squeezed hard in her chest at their open display of affection. They were so lucky to have found each other.

She cast a glance toward Levi from beneath her lashes, wondering if they would ever look at each other like Trace and Lily.

Yes, they'd made mad, passionate love through the night. Still, sex wasn't enough to declare undying love. They barely knew each other.

And if the Snakes had their way, Dallas and Levi wouldn't live for a repeat performance of the night's magic.

Dallas glanced around the table filled with laughter and the camaraderie she hadn't realized she'd missed from her time in the army. This group of former soldiers had managed to bring their brotherhood and devotion to each other with them to the civilian side. She envied their connection and enjoyed, for the moment, being included.

When the danger was over, and Levi went on to his next Outrider assignment, Dallas would go back to being a deputy sheriff and living alone.

Suddenly, she wasn't nearly as satisfied with life as she'd thought she was before she'd met Levi. Even through all the problems and near misses they'd had, she'd felt a connection, a sense of belonging she hadn't experienced since Brian's death. For that matter, since forever.

Being with Levi felt natural and…right.

LEVI STUDIED DALLAS out of the corner of his eye as she sat among the members of his team. She smiled, laughed and looked relaxed in their company. He suspected her time as an MP in the army made it easier for her to relate to others with a prior service background.

The thing that struck him the most was that she needed to smile more. She deserved to be happy. Levi realized he wanted to be a part of the reason Dallas smiled.

After the food was consumed, everyone helped clear the table.

Dallas filled a sink full of soapy water and started washing the dishes as the others brought them to her.

Rosalynn brought a stack of plates and laid them on the counter beside the sink. "I'll take over."

"I don't mind," Dallas said. "You and Lily cooked. It's the least I can do since you let me stay here last night."

"You don't have to earn your keep here. You've had a pretty tough couple of days. Don't you worry about us. One more plate isn't going to burden anyone."

"Mom's right," Trace said from behind Dallas. "Besides, I have a feeling it'll get worse with the Snakes before it gets better. You and Levi will have your work cut out for you today."

"And the team will, too." Levi topped off his mug of coffee and turned toward Trace. "Until this mess is resolved, we're counting on you,

Irish and Matt to be on call for the foreseeable future."

"Then we need to get it done," Trace said. "I have clients calling today. I expect we'll be stretched thin before we know it."

"I'm glad Becker is joining us. Have you heard from any of the others from our old team?" Irish asked.

Trace shook his head. "Rumblings, but nothing solid."

"Oh, yeah?" Levi cocked an eyebrow. "Who?"

A smile was Trace's answer. "Can't say until it's a sure thing."

Irish grinned and clapped his hands. "At this rate, we'll have the entire team working for the Outriders. It'll be like old times."

"Better." Trace slipped an arm around Lily and hugged her up against his side. "We'll have more of a life than we did on active duty."

"True," Irish said and pulled Tessa into his arms. "If I'd known what I was missing, I might have left the Deltas sooner."

Trace shook his head. "We left when we were ready. I like to think we made a difference while we were there."

Levi nodded, his memories flooding back. "We did."

Dallas stepped away from the sink, letting

Rosalynn take over. She wiped her hands on a dry dish towel and met Levi's gaze.

"Guess we'd better head to town and find out if Sheriff Greer had a chat with Billings and Langley last night," Dallas said.

Levi nodded. "Let's do it. The sooner we find the meth, the sooner we find out who's behind Harold Sims's death."

Dallas led the way out of the ranch house and climbed into her old truck.

Trace had followed them out and stood on the porch, his gaze taking in the ancient truck.

Levi shook his head. "Don't know why, but Dallas is attached to this wreck."

"It's old…not a wreck," Dallas called out. "And it gets us where we need to go."

Levi shrugged with a smile. "Unlike mine."

"I could loan you a truck until you have a chance to have yours fixed or replaced."

"Replaced," Levi said. "There's no fixing that burned-out hull."

Trace nodded. "I'll have a truck for you this afternoon. We'll bring it to you in town."

"Thank you." Levi climbed into the passenger seat of Dallas's pickup. "Not that there's anything wrong with your truck." He smiled across at her.

Her brow wrinkled. "I get it. My old truck is

an acquired taste. You'd prefer a younger, sexier model, I'm sure."

Levi nodded. "Definitely younger. And I kind of like air-conditioning."

Dallas laughed. "And here I thought you were a tough guy."

Levi puffed out his chest. "I *am* a tough guy. I just don't like snakes, and I enjoy a few creature comforts in my vehicles. I've had enough searing heat to last a lifetime."

"I get it," Dallas said. "I think I sweat my body weight in the first few days of the summer in Afghanistan."

"Another thing we have in common," Levi noted.

"What?" Dallas shifted into gear and headed down the gravel road that led off the ranch. "Sweating your body weight or enjoying creature comforts?"

He smiled. "That we've both deployed and understand the sacrifices our soldiers make to protect our country and freedoms."

She nodded, drove across the cattle guard and out onto the highway. "I think we've established that we have a lot in common."

"Yes, we have, and yes, we do."

"But isn't it true that opposites attract?" she asked, her gaze on the road ahead.

Levi studied her. "I think you have to have

a balance of things in common and things that make each of you unique in a relationship to make it interesting and to be compatible."

"And you have to be willing to accept each other for who you are without trying to change each other to fit," Dallas said.

"Was that how it was in your relationship with your fiancé? You accepted each other for who you were?"

She nodded. "I guess we did. We were friends to start with."

"Do you still love your fiancé?"

Dallas continued to stare straight forward. She paused for a moment before she answered.

"Yes, I do," she said. "Like you love a family member who's no longer with you. Like I said, we started out as friends, best friends. We knew each other for several years before we decided to get married. Losing him was like losing a family member, even though we weren't married. It hurt. A lot. But, eventually, the pain fades."

"And has it?" Levi asked.

She nodded. "Yes, it has."

"Do you think you'll ever be able to love again?"

She grinned and shot a glance at him. "Have you got someone in mind?"

He shrugged. "It was a hypothetical question."

"Hypothetically speaking," she started, "do you think *you* could trust yourself to love someone again?"

He grinned. "Do you have someone in mind?"

"I qualified the question with *hypothetically speaking.*"

He nodded. "I think if the right woman came along."

Dallas's brow twisted. "So, what you're saying is she hasn't come along yet?"

"I didn't say that," he said.

"So, you *have* found her?"

He tilted his head to one side. "I'm still trying to figure that out."

She nodded. "With the ink still drying on your divorce decree, I'm sure it's difficult to believe there might be someone out there you can trust with your heart."

He glanced forward. "That about sums it up."

"Then the question is," she said, "where do we fit? Is what we're doing a simple passing in the night?"

He turned to face her. "I hope not. I kind of like you."

She nodded, her attention still on the road ahead as they approached the outskirts of Whiskey Gulch. Finally, she turned toward him. "I kind of like you, too."

"Look out," Levi cried out. Out of the corner of his eye, a tow truck pulled out in front of them with a mangled car on the back.

Dallas turned her attention forward and slammed on the brakes, bringing her truck to a skidding halt, allowing the tow truck, with the vehicle on board, the right of way. She frowned. "Hey, isn't that Sean's sports car?"

Levi's eyes narrowed. "I was just thinking the same thing."

"Come on. Let's go see what the sheriff has to say."

The tow truck headed to the south side of town. Dallas pulled into the sheriff's station, shifted into Park and got out. Levi met her at the front of the truck, and they entered the sheriff's office at the same time.

Sheriff Greer was just hanging up the phone when he spotted them. "You were next on my list to call," he said. "I just got off the phone with the state crime scene investigators."

Before he could continue, Dallas blurted, "We saw Sean Langley's car being hauled off by a tow truck. What happened?"

"That's why I have the state investigators scheduled to come check out…the death of Sean Langley."

Dallas's eyes widened. "The what?"

"Marge Schubert, a waitress at the diner, reported that she had spotted a vehicle in the ditch on her way in to work this morning. She stopped to see if anybody was in it, and sure enough, she found Langley's body behind the wheel." The sheriff shook his head. "No pulse. He'd probably been dead for a couple of hours."

"Did he run off the road?" Dallas asked.

Even before the sheriff answered, Levi knew.

"No, he was run off the road. To be exact, he was shot, which caused him to run off the road. He was dead before his car wrecked into the ditch."

"Any idea who might have done it?" Levi asked.

The sheriff sighed. "Not yet."

"Did you have a chance to interview Langley and Billings last night at Sweeney's?"

The sheriff's lips pressed into a thin line. "When I'd got there, they'd already left. I was going to swing by the Billings place right after I'd made these calls."

The sheriff started for the door when the dispatcher called out, "Sheriff Greer, we have a disturbance at the feed store."

"What now?" he barked.

"A couple of ranch hands are throwing punches."

"Sheriff," Levi said, "we'll find Billings. You take that call."

"Good. He lives with his mother." The sheriff scribbled the address on a sheet of paper and handed it to Levi. "Good luck. He might be hard to find." Greer left the office, grumbling about cowboys behaving like children.

Dallas and Levi hurried into Dallas's old truck and headed out for the Billings residence, located a mile out of town.

Mrs. Billings answered on the first knock. "I'm not buying anything," she said as she opened the door.

"Mrs. Billings, I'm Deputy Warren." Levi flashed the star the sheriff had given him. "I'd like to speak to your son Evan."

"You and me both," she said. "You never know where that boy gets off to. He was supposed to feed the chickens this morning, but he never showed up. That's typical. Half the time he heads to Sweeney's Bar after he gets off work at the dance hall and stays until they close. But he usually comes home by three or four in the morning. He probably found him a girl."

"Would you happen to know which girl he might be with?" Dallas asked.

She shook her head. "No. That's just wishful thinking."

"Is there any place in particular he might have gone? Someplace he might want to hide?" Levi added.

Mrs. Billings frowned. "Is he in trouble with

the law again? Because you know, if he is, I'd be the first one to turn him in."

Dallas gave her a gentle smile. "We don't know yet. We have a few questions for him."

"He's been hanging out with that Sean Langley fella. The two of them together just spell trouble."

"Why do you say that, Mrs. Billings?" Dallas asked.

"Both of 'em spent the night in jail after they got high on something and made fools of themselves on Main Street. You'd think they'd learn their lesson."

"Have you known Evan and Sean to ever have any big disagreements with each other?" Levi asked.

"No. Those two are as thick as thieves. But who knows when two guys get together what they might argue over?" Her eyes narrowed. "Why do you ask? What's going on?"

"They found Sean's body in a ditch on the other side of town this morning. Someone had shot him."

Mrs. Billings's face paled. "And you think my boy did it?"

"We don't know, Mrs. Billings, but if he wasn't responsible, he might be next. We really need to find him."

"Oh, dear Lord." The woman clutched her hands to her chest and bent over.

Levi reached out and gripped her arm. "Are you okay, Mrs. Billings?"

"I need to sit. Can you help me to my chair?"

"Yes, ma'am." Levi circled an arm around her waist, walked her over to her chair and eased her into it.

"I can't believe that Evan would have shot his friend Sean. They've been friends since grade school. But if he didn't do it, that might mean someone else shot Sean and might go after my boy. Evan's in trouble."

Dallas nodded and knelt in front of Mrs. Billings. "It's possible. We really need to find Evan before something happens to him."

She shook her head slowly. "I don't know. I just don't know."

"Is there anywhere he would hide if he was scared?" Dallas asked. "Anyone he'd seek refuge with?"

"I don't know about *anybody*, but I do know when he got in trouble with his pa he'd hide in the woods. He had a fort behind the house."

Levi and Dallas both looked up at the same time through the window that had a view of the backyard.

Mrs. Billings shook her head. "Not at this house. The little house we had in town, back when his pa was alive. Evan had built a fort out of scrap lumber in one of the live oak trees on the ranch behind us. It might still be there."

"How far back in the woods was it?" Levi asked.

"For him, I'm sure it felt like a long way when he was little, but me and his pa found it pretty easily. It was due west of the little house, nestled in a thicket of live oak. The thicket is hard to miss. It's the only stand of trees in that field."

"Which house was it?" Dallas asked.

Mrs. Billings gave them the address. "When you find my boy, you tell him to get on home. I'll keep a shotgun by the door."

"Ma'am—" Levi touched her hand "—you might want to head into town and stay with a friend."

She blinked up at him. "Why?"

He took her hand in his. "Whoever shot Sean might come looking for Evan out here."

Her eyes widened. "You think they'd shoot me?"

"We don't know," Levi said, "but you'd be better off staying with a friend in town."

"Help me up, son, and grab my purse off the counter. I'll go visit my friend Barb."

"Take something for an overnight stay," Dallas insisted. "We don't know how long it will take to find Evan."

The older woman nodded, shuffled into her

bedroom and came out a few minutes later wheeling a small suitcase.

Dallas fetched her purse off the counter in the kitchen and together they got her out to her vehicle parked in the driveway. She was shaking when she turned the key in the ignition.

"Mrs. Billings?" Levi leaned into her open window. "Are you up to driving into town?"

She nodded. "I'll be okay."

He patted his hand on her car. "Okay, then. We'll follow you in."

"Thank you," she said. "And thank you for letting me know about Evan." The woman backed out of her driveway and drove the mile into town.

Levi and Dallas followed.

When Mrs. Billings turned right to go to her friend's house, they turned left on a narrow street and headed to the end, where there was a cul-de-sac. The house at the end of the street was a small cottage that had been boarded up and stood empty, another victim of a small town shrinking.

Based on Mrs. Billings's directions, they rounded the back of the house and set off directly west, walking into the brush and through tall grass where they could see a stand of live oak trees ahead. Some of the grass had been trampled, which gave Levi hope that they might find Evan in the stand of trees.

As they approached, they slowed. Levi put his arm out to stop Dallas from going farther. He pressed a finger to his lips and indicated she should get down in the grass. He squatted beside her. "He might be armed, and if he's scared, he could shoot. You cover me. I'll go in."

She shook her head. "I should be the one to go in."

"I'm good at this," he said. "I'm very quiet on my feet. Trust me."

Her lips pressed together for a moment and then she nodded. "I've got your back," she whispered.

He left her hiding in the grass and swung wide, hunkering low, letting the grass provide concealment until he could get close enough to the stand of trees to enter. Anyone else would be coming in from the direction of the house. He was entering from the rear of trees. He didn't see anything on the ground, but when he looked up, he saw a jumble of boards nailed to a live oak tree at the center of the stand. He crept forward, slipping from shadow to shadow until he was within fifteen feet of the tree.

Movement caught his eye. There definitely was somebody up in that tree. When he moved forward again, he stepped on a twig and it cracked, the sound accentuated in the silence of the forest.

"Who's there?" a voice called out. "Don't come any closer or I'll shoot."

Before he could say anything, Dallas's voice called out. "It's me, Deputy Jones. I just want to talk to you, Evan."

"I'm not talking to anyone," Evan shouted. "Go away."

"I can't do that," Dallas said. "I'm sure by now you know Sean's dead."

A curse sounded from the tree house. "That bastard killed him."

"Who, Evan?" Dallas asked.

"Where are you?" Evan demanded.

"Close," she said.

"Step out into the open."

Levi shook his head and murmured, "Oh, hell no."

"I'm not gonna do that, Evan, not until you throw down your weapon."

"No way," Evan said. "I need it. He shot Sean. He's coming for me next."

"Who's coming for you, Evan?" Dallas asked.

"The man who shot Sean."

"Tell me who that is, so we can find him and take him in so he doesn't do the same to you."

"I don't know who it is." Evan's voice shook. "He wore a Halloween mask."

"Did you recognize his voice?"

"No, I didn't. He disguised his voice." Evan's voice faded. "It was supposed to have been a quick sale."

"Of the meth you stole from the Snakes' stash?" Dallas pressed.

Levi crept closer. Hell, he was standing beneath the tree. He could see Evan beneath the gaps in the slats that had been nailed to the tree. He was facing in the direction of Dallas's voice.

Levi studied the fort. Some of the boards hung loose, with only one nail keeping them from falling to the ground, which left a gap near the rear large enough for Levi to swing up into it. He just needed Dallas to keep Evan's attention long enough so that he could get in and disarm the man.

"I didn't steal that stash," Evan insisted.

"No, but you're selling it. So, who stole it?" Dallas persisted. "Was it Sean?"

Evan shook his head. "No, Sean didn't steal it, either."

"Then how did you get ahold of some to sell?"

"From someone else."

"Tell me," Dallas urged.

Evan snorted. "The guy I always buy my stuff from."

"And who's that?"

Evan threw a hand in the air. "I can't tell you that."

"Why? Will he kill you?" Dallas asked.

"No, I can't tell you because he shows up in a black ski mask. We hand him the money…he hands us the stash."

"Where do these transactions take place?" Dallas asked.

Levi bunched his muscles, reached up, gripped a thick tree branch and waited for Evan to start talking.

"Behind Sweeney's Bar," Evan said.

Levi swung up into the tree, landed on the floor of the tree house, barreled into Evan and knocked the weapon from his hands.

The young man slammed into the side of the tree house. The boards cracked and gave way, and he fell to the ground next to the gun. Evan got his hand around the pistol's grip, rolled onto his back and pointed the weapon at Levi.

Levi was already flying out of the tree house. He landed on top of the young man and held up his hands. "Don't shoot."

"I knew I shouldn't have trusted you." Evan snarled.

Dallas came running, her weapon drawn. "Drop it, Evan. Levi isn't here to hurt you."

Evan kept his gun trained on Levi. "If he

wasn't here to hurt me, then why'd he knock me out of the tree house?"

"To protect me," she answered. "Put your gun down."

He held it pointed at Levi's face even as Levi straddled him, keeping him from rising. Levi's arm was cocked and ready to bat the gun out of Evan's hand. He trained his gaze on the boy's trigger finger. If he so much as twitched, Levi would have that gun out of his hand so fast he wouldn't know what hit him.

"Put the gun down, Evan," Dallas said, her voice soft. "We know you're scared. You should be. Whoever killed Sean will be after you next. You need to tell us anything you know so we can find who's responsible."

"I told you everything I know. We were supposed to make a sale in that quarry, but the guy who came showed up in a Halloween mask and threatened us."

"Give me the gun, Evan," Dallas said and reached her hand out.

He hesitated a minute more, but then passed the weapon to Dallas.

Levi let go of the breath he'd been holding, stood and pulled the young man to his feet.

Dallas tucked Evan's gun into the waistband of her jeans. "How did he threaten you?"

"He said that if we didn't kill the man who'd

sold us the meth, he'd kill us. We went back to Sweeney's Bar, hoping to run into the man who'd sold us the meth. He never showed up. But then, he only shows up every other night. I headed home. Sean got in his car and left the bar. I got a call from a friend early this morning saying that Sean's body had been found. As soon as I heard that, I left my mom's house and ran."

"Were you going to kill your supplier?" Dallas asked.

Evan shook his head. "No, I was going to warn him."

"Was Sean going to kill him?"

"No," Evan said. "We talked about it. We thought the guy would give us a little time to do the deed. By then, we might be able to get out of town. Sean was going to go to his place, pack a few things and then come back and get me in the morning."

"How often did you get product from your guy behind Sweeney's Bar?" Levi asked.

"Every other night," Evan said. "Last night was not one of our nights. We'd gotten it the night before."

"So, your guy might show up tonight?"

"He might or he might not. Everybody will have heard of Sean's death before the end of the day. For all I know, my supplier might ghost."

"Makes sense," Levi said. "If he stole the stash from the Snakes, he's in big trouble. They'll want it back, and they might think you have it."

"That's what I'm afraid of," Evan said. He looked from Dallas to Levi. "So, what are you gonna do with me?"

"I think it's best if I arrest you," Dallas said.

"And lock me up in jail?" Evan asked, his voice almost hopeful.

Dallas nodded. "I think that might be the safest place for you right now, but maybe not here in Whiskey Gulch."

"I'd be okay with getting the hell out of here," he said. "Even if it means going to jail."

"Come on. Let's get you back to town." Levi gripped the young man's arm and strode through the trees.

Dallas walked on the other side of Evan. "Do I need to cuff you?"

Evan shook his head. "You don't have to, but if you want to you can."

She shook her head. "Just hold your hands behind your back and pretend you're cuffed. That way if anyone sees you, they'll think you're being hauled in on criminal charges."

He nodded, his eyes filling with tears. "Sean's dead."

Levi nodded. "Let's make sure you're not next."

Chapter Thirteen

Dallas and Levi transported Billings back to the sheriff's office and, since they were short-staffed, helped process him in.

The sheriff was still out at the feed store breaking up the brawl.

Because she was still officially on administrative leave, Dallas did all the paperwork and had Levi sign off.

One of the deputies loaded Evan into an unmarked vehicle for transport to San Antonio, where he would be held until his court date.

Evan had readily confessed to selling drugs. "It beats being shot to death by whoever killed Sean."

They did their best to sneak him in and out of the sheriff's station so that nobody else would know that they had found him, especially his supplier and whoever had killed Sean, considering they weren't one and the same. The fewer people who knew where Evan was, the better.

By the time they had Evan safely out of Whiskey Gulch, it was well into the afternoon. Neither one of them had eaten.

"You want to catch a sandwich at the diner?" Levi asked.

"Sounds good. We might need some fortitude for the rest of the day." Dallas sighed and climbed into her truck. "I have a feeling it's going to be a long one."

The diner was fairly empty at that time of day, with only a couple of locals drinking coffee at the counter and one older man finishing off a sandwich.

Levi led Dallas to the booth in the corner they had occupied the last time they had been there. Jess came out of the kitchen with a stack of napkins. "Oh…it's you two. Give me a second," she said. After she'd stuffed napkins into one of the napkin holders, she pulled a pad and paper out of her apron pocket and crossed to their table. "What can I get you deputies?" she asked. "Coffee?"

"Is the kitchen closed?" Levi looked over her shoulder toward the swinging door. "We're hungry."

"Not at all," she answered. "The chef can have a sandwich made up in no time, or if you'd rather have a hamburger and french fries, he can do that, too. However, he hasn't started serving the dinner menu yet."

"That's fine. Actually, a hamburger and french fries would be great," Levi said.

Dallas nodded. "Make that two."

Jess carried their order to the kitchen and came back with a pitcher full of ice water and poured a couple of glasses for them.

"I would like that coffee as well, if you don't mind," Levi said.

"Sure." She left and came back a moment later with a couple of mugs and a coffee carafe. After she poured the coffee in the mugs, she hesitated. "Did you find the guys who were selling the stolen meth?" She didn't wait for their response but went on to say, "Was it Sean Langley? I heard he was shot and killed this morning."

"We can't say," Dallas said.

"Was the shooting drug related?" Jess asked.

Dallas grimaced. "Again, we can't say."

Jess shook her head. "I knew it. I need to get away from this town. Dylan needs to get away with me. We'll never be safe here. I'm not raising my baby here."

"Whiskey Gulch isn't a bad place to raise a child," Dallas said. "It's just some of the people make it difficult for others."

Jess snorted. "Difficult? Try deadly. As far

as I can tell, that motorcycle gang, the Snakes, calls the shots, and if you're on the wrong side of the barrel, you're dead. As far as Dylan's concerned, the baby and I could be used as leverage to keep him in place. Our only option is to get the heck out of here, change our names and start over somewhere else."

"I'm sorry you feel that way," Dallas said.

She crossed her arms over her chest. "It's your job to make sure this doesn't continue. What have you done to stop them?"

Dallas nodded. "We can't do it without help. We need witnesses, and we need to know where they moved the meth house so we can catch those responsible for cooking it up, but we have to catch them red-handed to put them away."

Jess shook her head. "Nobody's going to nark on anyone in the Snakes' gang. Anyone who does will end up like Sean, for that matter." Jess glanced out the window. "Has anyone seen Evan Billings? He and Sean were always together. I'll bet you find him in a ditch next."

Dallas didn't say anything. She couldn't reveal that she knew where Evan was, and that he was on his way to San Antonio to jail, where they hoped he'd stay safe from the Snakes. Dallas leaned forward and lowered her voice. "Jess, you can help us."

Jess frowned. "How can I help you?"

"If you hear anything," Dallas said, "let us know. Give us a heads-up."

"Anything like what?"

"Like where we can find the Snakes' hideout. Where Johnny Marks might be staying. Who shot Sean? Any little thing you can come up with. It might seem small, but it could lead us to the bigger fish."

"I can't nark. I live here." Jess rested a hand over her flat belly. "The sad thing is that we can't afford to leave Whiskey Gulch, not yet. We don't have enough money to fix the car or to even find a new place to live. We're kind of stuck here."

"All the more reason to help us stop what the gang is doing," Dallas said.

Jess nodded. "I get what you're saying. I just don't think I can help."

"Order up!" the chef called from the kitchen.

Jess spun, hurried back to the kitchen and returned with their tray full of food. After laying the plates out on the table, she went back to work, stuffing napkins into napkin holders and filling condiment containers with salt, pepper and ketchup.

Dallas picked up her hamburger and took a bite, no longer that hungry but determined to provide her body with the fuel that she might need for that evening. "Jess and Dylan have so many strikes against them. Bringing a baby into the world is going to make it even harder."

"If they really care about each other," Levi said, "they'll make it work. Hopefully the baby will help them to realize every decision matters in life, and they need to make good ones. Sometimes," Levi said, "making good decisions comes with maturity."

"Yeah, that baby is gonna make them mature really fast. If not, I hope they give it up for adoption to somebody who will take care of it."

Levi's gaze followed Jess. Every so often she touched her belly, where the baby was still too small to even show a bump. The woman appeared to care enough to be worried about the future of her child.

"Somehow," Levi said, "we need to resolve the situation with the Snakes. They can't continue to run the county and terrorize its citizens."

Dallas gave a wry grin. "And to think it all started with Judd Marks when he wanted to start a motorcycle club for people that just enjoyed riding."

"Yeah," Levi said, "it's sad that his brothers made it something that Judd Marks probably never had intended."

Dallas and Levi were just finishing up their hamburger and french fries and their second cup of coffee when Dylan came in through the kitchen and out into the dining room. He stood at the swinging door and waved for Jess to come to him.

The waitress frowned. "What are you doing here?"

He waved her toward him. "Jess, I need to talk to you."

She glanced around and then joined him near the swinging door. They put their heads together, and he whispered, his face intense. A frown furrowed his brow.

Jess shook her head. "Just don't go."

At least, that was how Dallas read her lips.

Dylan glanced over her shoulder to where Dallas and Levi sat in the corner booth, and he frowned heavily. He drew Jess into the kitchen and the door swung shut behind them.

"I wonder what he was so frantic about," Levi said.

"Yeah, me too." Dallas started to get out of her chair to go find out, when Jess reappeared alone, her face flushed. She brought their bill to their table.

"Everything okay, Jess?" Dallas asked.

"Yeah, sure," she said. "Everything's just fine."

By the way she said it, Dallas knew it wasn't fine. "Jess, if you're in trouble, let us know."

She shook her head. "I'm not."

"Do you want to talk about it?" Dallas asked.

Jess shook her head. "No. I can't. No one's safe in this town, especially people who talk."

Dallas held her hand. "Let me have your pen."

Jess handed over the pen.

Dallas wrote her cell phone number on a napkin. "If you change your mind, call me. If you need someone to talk to, or have anything that can help us to resolve this situation, call. I don't care what time. Just do it."

Jess stuffed the napkin into her apron pocket and turned away.

Levi paid the bill, and the two left the diner, climbed into Dallas's truck and headed back to the sheriff's office.

The sheriff was back and looking tired. "Anyone who's ever said that women are hard to work with has never dealt with a bunch of angry cowboys."

"How'd that go?" Dallas asked.

"Everyone went home, except for the ones who went to the clinic for broken noses and broken ribs." The sheriff's mouth twisted. "The good news is they'll all live to fight another day."

"What started it?" Dallas asked.

The sheriff rubbed a hand through his hair and said, "I don't know, and frankly, I don't care. It's done. Now, tell me what happened with Evan Billings."

They filled him in on what they'd done with Billings and how they'd sent him to San Antonio for safekeeping.

"So, what's your next course of action?" he asked.

Dallas met Levi's gaze. "Billings said he would meet with his supplier behind Sweeney's Bar. I think it might be worth our time to go investigate."

Sheriff Greer's eyes narrowed. "Sweeney won't let you do anything without a court order."

"We didn't plan on asking Sweeney's permission, or, at least, I didn't," Dallas said.

The corners of Levi's mouth twitched. "You don't like that guy very much, do you?"

"Not particularly," Dallas said. "But someone was supplying Billings behind the bar. I think it might be worth looking around to see if maybe that stash is hidden somewhere around there. I seriously doubt it, but it doesn't hurt to look."

"You think Sweeney might have something to do with that stolen meth?" Sheriff Greer asked.

Dallas shrugged. "I don't know. At this point I don't know anything, except that somebody was supplying Evan and Sean, and that somebody else wanted that supplier dead. We need some kind of clue to find out who those two people are. It might lead to that stolen meth and also to our killer. Or killers, depending on how many people it took to beat Harold and then shoot Sean. Either way, we're going to be at Sweeney's Bar tonight."

The sheriff nodded. "Well, be careful and call for backup if you need it."

"Yes, sir," Dallas said.

"Now, I'm going home to have dinner." Sheriff Greer settled his uniform cowboy hat on his head. "I have a feeling it's going to be a long night."

Dallas and Levi went to Sean's home, where he'd lived in a garage apartment. Other than drug paraphernalia, there wasn't much else to go on. They searched the entire apartment in less than twenty minutes and came up with nothing. If he'd stolen the meth, it wasn't there. Truthfully, Dallas hadn't really expected it to be there. But she'd hoped that there would be a clue as to who was dealing the meth.

As the shadows grew longer, Dallas and Levi headed toward Sweeney's Bar. Dallas didn't want to get there too early. She preferred to go in after dark when the bar was busy, and nobody would notice them coming or going. On the way, they stopped by the sheriff's station one more time. The sheriff wasn't there, but they did learn from the deputy that had gone to San Antonio that he'd made it there safely with Evan Billings.

The young drug dealer had been placed in a cell by himself, away from others, just in case the motorcycle club had connections all the way in San Antonio.

Dallas and Levi sat in the interrogation room, which was nothing more than four walls, a conference table and a couple of chairs. They disassembled their handguns, cleaned them and reassembled them, filling their magazines with bullets.

By nine o'clock, Dallas looked across at Levi. "You ready?"

He nodded. "Let's do this."

She drove her pickup to within a block of Sweeney's Bar and parked it in the alley beside a flower shop. "We'll walk from here." She patted her gun beneath the jacket she wore, slipped her cell phone into her bra and pulled it out again. "You know, it might be a good thing if we were able to follow each other's cell phones in case something happens and we're split up. My cell phone goes with me everywhere."

"I agree." Levi pulled his phone out of his back pocket.

Dallas leaned close to him. "I have this app on my phone." She showed him the app, and he downloaded it onto his phone. "The sheriff has my cell phone on his location app as well."

"Just don't get lost, okay?" Levi said, his brow furrowing.

She smiled. "I don't plan on it, but if I did, would you miss me?"

He pulled her into his arms and stared into her eyes from the light shining down from a streetlamp. "Yes, I would miss you."

Her lips twisted into a wry grin. "We only just got to know each other."

"Yeah, and I like what I know." He brushed a strand of her hair away from her cheek. "And I want to get to know you even better."

She rested her hands on his chest. "Well, let's not do anything stupid tonight."

"I'm all for that." Levi crushed her lips with his in a kiss that curled Dallas's toes. When he came back up for air, he stared down into her eyes and said, "Do you think there's a chance that what we are feeling for each other could be real?"

She laughed. "I hope so."

He smiled and kissed the tip of her nose. "I hope so, too. We have so much in common."

She laughed. "You and your common stuff. Did you not have anything in common with your ex-wife?"

He nodded. "We went to the same high school.

We had some of the same friends, but that was about it. She was not in love with the army, and she never liked being a part of it. I, on the other hand, liked being a part of something bigger than me...of serving my country and being there for my brothers and sisters in arms."

"I loved being in the army, except for the part where you lose friends in battle. I guess that makes me different from her, which is a good thing, right?"

Levi nodded. "Absolutely. You're strong. You're courageous. You served your country. That's more than a lot of people would do. I admire that."

Dallas grimaced. "Most guys find that intimidating."

His arms tightened around her. "Most guys aren't me."

"That's for damn sure." She leaned up on her toes and pressed a kiss to his lips.

He returned the pressure by crushing her in his arms and kissing her until she was breathless. When he finally let her breathe, he lifted his head. "Okay, so what's the plan?"

She laughed, smoothed her hair and then took a deep breath. "I want to look around outside the bar and see if there's any kind of clue as to who Evan's supplier is."

"Are you thinking it might be Sweeney himself?"

"I don't know." Dallas frowned. "It doesn't make sense. He has a bar. Why would he risk losing his bar over selling drugs, and why would he risk his life selling stolen meth, when everybody knows the Snakes can be ruthless?"

"No, it doesn't make sense," Levi said. "But then, anybody who deals with meth doesn't make a whole lot of sense."

Dallas nodded. "So, we start at the back of the bar, where Evan Billings made his deals with the man in the mask."

Levi nodded and set out, moving in the back alley behind the storefronts, keeping to the shadows, until they reached the back of Sweeney's Bar. The only thing behind the bar was Sweeney's four-door sedan, a large trash bin, a stack of broken-down cardboard boxes and a recycle bin full of bottles. They poked around the cardboard boxes, the recycle bin, and even looked inside the trash bin. They would have checked the interior of Sweeney's car, but the doors were locked.

"I'm going to get my slim jim from my truck," Dallas said.

"I'm coming with you," Levi said.

Dallas shook her head. "You don't need to. I'll be right back."

"Sorry, it's not up for discussion. I'm going with you." He cupped her elbow and started back to where they'd parked her truck.

Dallas grabbed the slim jim, and they were back behind Sweeney's Bar within two minutes.

As they approached, the rear door opened, and Sweeney came out.

Dallas and Levi ducked around the side of the bar. Dallas edged close and peered around the corner of the building.

Sweeney unlocked his car, got in and drove off.

"Well, we won't get to see what's inside his car," Levi said, "but now would be a good time to go in and check out his office."

"Let's do it," Dallas agreed.

He stuck out his arm to keep her from following through. "*I'll* go in. I need somebody out here to let me know when Sweeney gets back so I can get out before he comes back into his office."

"Let me go in," Dallas said. "You stand guard."

"If anyone gets caught, I'd rather it was me. You'd lose your job. I'd just lose my star." He grinned. "Promise me you'll stay out of sight. I don't want you getting hurt."

"I will."

"Good. Now, be sure to warn me if Sweeney comes back. Just text me. I'll have it on vibrate."

She nodded. "Hurry up. He might not have gone far."

"On it." He tried the handle on the back door. When it didn't turn, he looked toward her. "Going around the front. You need to hide."

She nodded and ducked into the shadow of the trash bin.

Levi slipped around the side of the bar and out of sight.

Dallas didn't like cooling her heels in the dark, but Levi was right. He needed to be fore-warned if Sweeney returned before he came back out.

While she waited, she thought about Levi and the kiss they'd shared, and she smiled. He liked her, and she sure liked him. The more she thought about it, the more she realized how much she liked him. Could she be falling in love?

After losing Brian, she wasn't sure she'd ever want to fall in love again. It was heartbreaking when you lost somebody you cared about. Then again, life wasn't worth living unless you had those feelings and those amazing moments of happiness to make up for all the sorrow. And she truly felt happy when she was with Levi. He made her feel things she'd never felt with Brian. She wanted to feel those again—in fact, she wanted to feel those going to bed at night and waking up every morning. She wanted the chance to explore what their relationship meant and if it could stand the test of time.

Headlights shone around the corner of the bar.

Dallas tensed.

Sweeney's sedan pulled in and parked beside the trash bin.

Her pulse racing, Dallas quickly texted Levi, letting him know Sweeney was back. Because Sweeney was going in through the back door, Levi would have to exit through the front.

Once Sweeney entered the back door, Dallas saw her moment to check out Sweeney's sedan. She abandoned her hiding place next to the trash bin.

She slid the slim jim between the window and the door on the passenger side, fished around a bit and unlocked the door.

She quickly checked the glove box, the console, and shone her cell phone light under the seats. Other than food wrappings and trash, she didn't find anything. All she had left to check was the trunk.

Dallas found the lever under the dash on the driver's side and tripped it. The trunk popped open. She ran around to the back, praying Sweeney wasn't going to leave the bar again anytime soon. She leaned into the trunk and found a couple of empty cardboard liquor boxes and a gym bag. She lifted the gym bag. It was heavier than what a gym bag would be with just standard workout wear. She unzipped it and shone her cell phone light down at a dozen plastic bags filled with something white. One of the packages had been torn open.

Dallas's heart skipped several beats. This was it. This had to be the stolen meth. She turned off her flashlight and reached up to close the trunk when something hit her head from behind. Pain shot through her skull, blinding her. Then someone shoved her from behind. She fell into the trunk. Her legs were lifted inside, and the trunk lid closed. Trapped inside, her head screaming in pain, Dallas blacked out.

LEVI HAD MADE good headway in Sweeney's office, going through the file cabinets, checking through the desk drawers. He'd come across a drawer that was locked and was working on jimmying the lock when his cell phone vibrated. He glanced down.

He's back

Levi had just popped the lock on the drawer when he heard the back door open. With nowhere to hide but a small closet in the office, he stepped into it and pulled the door closed. He prayed Sweeney was needed in the bar and wouldn't stay long in his office.

The back door slammed shut. Footsteps sounded in the hallway and entered the office. Something was tossed onto the desk, and then footsteps sounded again, headed toward the bar. Levi was about to step out of the closet and dive for the exit when footsteps returned.

He closed the closet door, leaving just enough of a gap so that he could see out.

Sweeney entered his office, grabbed what he'd thrown onto the desk and headed back out the rear exit.

Knowing he only had seconds to spare in case Sweeney turned around and came right back in, Levi left the closet, opened the drawer he'd popped the lock on and stared down at a dark ski mask that would cover a man's head and only expose his eyes and mouth.

Bingo.

Sweeney was the supplier selling to Billings and Sean. He was also the seller somebody wanted dead. He had to have been the one who stole the meth and beat poor Harold Sims to death.

Levi quickly closed the door, left the office, passed through the front of the bar and left. He made a wide circle and came around to the rear of the bar.

Sweeney's car was gone.

"Dallas," he whispered. When she didn't respond, he called out a little louder. "Dallas." His pulse quickened, his heart thudding against his chest. "Dallas?" He looked behind the trash bin, glanced inside it and then checked around the opposite corner of the bar from where he'd been. He quickly realized Dallas wasn't there.

He made a complete circle around the bar, hoping, but not expecting, to find her. He ran back to where they had parked the truck. She wasn't there. He couldn't even take the truck. Her keys were with her.

He texted her.

She didn't respond.

He called her.

Again, she didn't respond. She probably had her cell phone on silent.

Levi ran back to the bar. As he ran, he dialed the sheriff's office and asked to speak to Sheriff Greer. When the man came on the line, he said, "She's gone."

"Who's gone?" the sheriff asked.

"Deputy Jones." He explained what had happened.

The sheriff swore. "You think Sweeney got her?"

"I don't know," Levi said, a sick feeling lodging in his gut. "But it has to be."

"We have to find her before he hurts her."

If he hasn't already, Levi thought.

The sheriff continued. "I'll put out a BOLO for Sweeney's sedan."

"Let me know what you find." Levi's jaw hardened as he kicked into battle mode. "In the meantime, I'm calling in my team."

"Good," the sheriff said. "We could use all the help we can get."

Levi checked one more time all around the bar and inside as well. He didn't find Dallas. He was dialing Trace Travis's number as he walked out of the bar and almost ran into Jess.

Her eyes were wide, her face drawn. "Oh, thank God I found you. I tried to call Deputy Jones, but she didn't answer."

"What's wrong, Jess?" Though he was more worried about Dallas, Levi stopped to listen to the pregnant woman.

"It's Dylan. The Snakes are having a big rendezvous out at the quarry. I don't know what's going to happen, but Dylan sounded scared."

"If he was scared, why did he go?"

"He was afraid that if he didn't, they'd kill him." She grimaced. "As it is, they might kill him anyway."

"The quarry?" Levi asked.

Jess nodded. "Yes."

Then Levi remembered he'd added Dallas's phone to his finder app. Levi checked the app for Dallas's cell phone location. It was on the move, headed in the direction of the quarry. His stomach clenched.

If Sweeney was taking Dallas out to the Snakes' rendezvous, Johnny would shoot her for killing his brother. Levi couldn't let that happen. "What time were they meeting at the quarry?"

"I don't know," Jess said. "He was headed out there a few minutes ago." She held out her hand with a wad of bills in it. "He gave me this. He said if he didn't come back, to use it to buy a bus ticket out of Whiskey Gulch."

Chapter Fourteen

Jess touched Levi's arm. "Are you going out there?"

Levi covered her hand with his. "Yes, but I'm not going alone."

"I'm going with you," Jess said.

Levi shook his head. "No, you're not. You're going to go someplace safe. I suggest you go to the sheriff's home and stay there with his wife. Do you have transportation?"

She nodded. "I have my bicycle."

Levi frowned. "Do you know where the sheriff lives?"

She nodded. "Yes, I do."

"Go straight there, don't stop, don't talk to anybody. Just go straight there and stay."

Tears filled her eyes. "What about Dylan? I don't want my baby growing up without a father."

"I'll take care of him," Levi promised. "Right now, you need to take care of yourself and your baby."

She nodded and walked to where she had left her bicycle, picked it up off the ground, got on and rode away.

Levi hoped she reached the Greers' residence safely. He would have accompanied her, if Dallas wasn't missing and most likely in danger. He called Trace Travis.

"Travis here," Trace answered.

"This is Levi," he said. "I need the team."

"You got it," Trace said. "Where are you?"

Levi's fist clenched. "I'm at Sweeney's Bar. I lost Dallas."

Trace muttered a curse. "We'll be there in fifteen."

"Make it sooner and come armed."

The sheriff arrived at Sweeney's Bar before Trace and the Outrider team. Levi took the sheriff into Sweeney's office and showed him what he'd found in the drawer. That plus Billings's testimony about purchasing drugs from a man with a ski mask painted Sweeney as their guy who had been selling the stolen meth through Billings and Langley.

The sheriff took a picture of the evidence and then bagged it and stowed it in his vehicle.

By that time, Trace, Irish and Matt arrived in Trace's truck, and the sheriff had already called in the only other deputy on duty. The men met in the parking lot of Sweeney's Bar.

They agreed they'd head for the quarry. Before they reached the turnoff, they'd park half a mile away and go in on foot. The sheriff deputized the team, but also warned them not to shoot unless they were fired on first.

Levi nodded, but he'd use his own judgment. If Dallas's life, his, or any member of his team was in danger, he'd shoot first.

They loaded up and drove out of town on the highway leading to the quarry. As planned, a half mile from the quarry's entrance, they parked their vehicles in the bushes and got out.

Trace had equipped each member of the team with a communications headset. He had two extras for the deputy and the sheriff.

"Let me go in first," Levi said. "I'll do what I can to locate Dallas before the rest of you get too close and they find out we're onto them."

The sheriff frowned. "I should be the one to go in first."

Levi shook his head. "This is what I trained for, to infiltrate without being detected."

Trace nodded. "Levi's the lightest on his feet. He can get within three feet of the enemy and they'd never know he was there."

The sheriff narrowed his eyes for a moment, then nodded. "I can't make that same claim. You're first in. We'll wait for you to give us the go-ahead."

"Just remember," Levi said, "Sweeney has Dallas. If there's any shooting to be done, make sure she doesn't get caught in the cross fire. And Dylan's out there. He doesn't want to be, but he has to be. Try not to shoot him as well. He's got a baby on the way."

They moved out, picking their way through the underbrush in the trees until they reached a point where Levi held up his fist. He'd go on alone from that point. The others would stand down until he located Dallas.

Levi moved on toward the quarry. When he was within a hundred yards of his destination, he could see the lights shining from more than a dozen motorcycles and one car... Sweeney's four-door sedan.

"I see them," he said into his headset. "I'm going in closer."

"Don't try to take them on by yourself," Trace warned. "Let us know when we can get close enough to cover you."

Sticking to the shadows, Levi moved in closer. He got into a position as near as he could to the people standing in the quarry. Any closer, and he'd have to step out into the open. From where he stood, he could hear most of the conversation going on between members of the Snakes, especially since it appeared to be a shouting match.

A dark-haired man with broad shoulders and a barrel chest stood toe to toe with a thinner man with long greasy blond hair and a bandanna tied around his head. He recognized the man with the dark hair as Marcus, the guy who'd beat up Dylan.

Nowhere within the circle of motorcycle riders did Levi see even a hint of Dallas. Sweeney's car was there. The finder app showed her location nearby. But where?

Marcus puffed out his chest and glared down at the one with the greasy blond hair. "Where's the product?"

"I tell ya, Marcus, I don't know," the man replied.

"Johnny Marks, you're lying. You and your brother have been siphoning off the stash for some time now."

Johnny crossed his arms over his chest. "You can't prove that, and why would I steal from my own people?"

Marcus sneered. "Because you're just like your brother was…selfish and greedy. You don't like to share, and that's why you killed Sean."

"I don't know what you're talking about," Johnny said.

Marcus pulled a gun and aimed it at Johnny's head. "Do you know what I'm talking about now?"

Johnny raised his hands. "Hey, dude, we're on the same team."

Marcus shook his head. "No, we're not. We haven't been on the same team since we set up shop. I've been watching you, and I set up a camera. I know it was you that took the stash of product. We want it back, and we want it back now."

Still holding up his hands, Johnny said, "I can't give you what I don't have."

"Then you better find it quick. Our buyer is threatening to kill all of us if he doesn't get his product in the next twenty-four hours."

Johnny shrugged. "I don't have it."

"You can't tell me you sold all of that in this short amount of time."

"I can't tell you I did anything with it because I don't have it," Johnny insisted.

"Then who'd you give it to? Because somebody's been distributing in the area through Sean Langley and Evan Billings."

"Maybe you should talk to them," Johnny said.

Marcus shook his head. "That's kind of hard to do when one of them is dead, as I'm sure you know. I'm betting the cops will match your gun to the bullet that killed Sean."

Johnny pulled the gun from the holster around

his shoulders and pushed it toward Marcus. "I didn't do it. You got the wrong guy."

"We know you stole the stuff." Marcus held the gun steadily pointed at Johnny's head. "The question is, how did Harold Sims get involved, and why did you have to go and kill him?"

"I didn't kill him," Johnny said. "That deputy did."

"After you beat him and left him for dead."

"Again, I don't know what you're talking about."

"Oh, yeah, we know somebody who would beg to differ."

The barrel-chested man jerked his head. "Bring her out."

A woman was dragged out, held between two other big guys. She kicked and screamed the whole way.

Levi tensed until he realized it wasn't Dallas, but another woman with bleached-blond hair, a low-cut blouse and tight jeans.

"Let me go," she yelled. "I ain't got nothing to do with anything. I didn't steal no meth."

"We don't think you did, but you know who did."

The woman stopped struggling and stared across at Johnny Marks. Her eyes narrowed. She raised a finger and pointed at the man. "He done it. He stole the meth from that hunting cabin."

"And how do you know this?" Marcus asked.

She gave a bark of laughter. "He was bragging about it when we were in bed. Said he got a big ole bunch of it, but the cheap bastard wouldn't give me any of it."

The barrel-chested man turned toward Johnny.

Johnny shook his head. "You gonna believe a crazy woman? How do you know she ain't lying?"

"How do I know you're not lying?" Marcus asked.

"Why would I lie to my people? Why would I lie to my gang?" Johnny said.

"If you're my people, you'll tell me. You demand loyalty from everybody else, but you don't give it. Tell us where it is, or I'm gonna kill you here and now."

Johnny frowned. "I don't have it."

"Wrong answer." The barrel-chested man raised his gun and shot Johnny in the arm.

"Damn," Levi murmured.

"What happened?" the sheriff asked.

"Marcus shot Johnny."

"That's it," the sheriff said. "We have to go in."

"We can't. Not until we know where Dallas is."

"I can't stand by and let these people kill each other," Sheriff Greer said.

"We can't come out until we know Dallas is safe. He didn't kill Johnny, just wounded him."

Johnny yelled. "Now, why did you have to go and do that?" He grabbed his arm to stem the bleeding. "I told you, I don't have it."

"You better find it before I shoot the other arm."

"I don't have it because—"

A shot rang out. Everyone ducked. Johnny clenched his chest, and his eyes rounded. He dropped to his knees and then fell forward, landing on his face.

"What's going on?" Trace Travis asked into Levi's ear.

"Snakes rotting from within," Levi responded in a whisper.

"Any sign of Dallas?" the sheriff asked.

"No," Levi responded.

"You shot Johnny!" One of the other motorcycle club members who'd stood by thus far stepped closer to the man who'd shot Johnny. "You had no right."

"Yeah, well, maybe you were in cahoots with him?" The guy raised his gun and shot the man.

"Now would be a good time for the team to converge," Levi said into his headset.

"Have you found Dallas?" the sheriff asked.

"No, but this situation is imploding as I speak."

"On our way in," Trace said.

Levi spotted Dylan on the edge of the group of motorcycle riders. He squatted in the dust, probably to keep his head down when the bullets started flying again.

"None of this would have happened," another man said, "if Judd Marks had stayed."

"What are you saying?" Marcus demanded. "Well, he ain't here now, is he? Johnny and Jimmy betrayed us. I guess that makes me in charge now. You got a problem with that?"

The man shook his head. "No. I just meant Judd didn't set this club up to push drugs."

"Again," Marcus said, as if to a dull child, "Judd ain't here. If you have a problem with how things work now…" He waved his gun.

"Leave him alone, Marcus," another member said. "Leave him alone."

"I'm tired of the lies," Marcus said. "And I'm tired of people stealing from the rest of us. Whoever has that meth better give it back now, or more people are going to die here tonight." He pointed his gun at one of the other members of the motorcycle gang. "Was it you, Ross?"

Ross shook his head. "No, it wasn't me, and don't point that gun if you're not gonna use it."

Marcus pointed it at the man who'd just told him not to. "What you all don't understand is we have a customer who has paid for this batch.

If he doesn't get it within the next twenty-four hours, it won't matter if I shoot you now because they will kill us later anyway."

"Give them back their money," another man said.

"I can't," Marcus said. "Johnny and Jimmy spent it."

"Marcus, put that gun down," another man said. "Shooting our people won't solve this problem."

"I'm not putting my weapon down until whoever has that meth coughs it up."

The man who'd told him to put his weapon down pulled his own gun and shot Marcus. Then it became a free-for-all, with different members of the team shooting at others.

Levi stayed low, as low as he could get against the ground as the bullets flew. He prayed wherever Dallas was that she didn't get hit by one. Members of the motorcycle club climbed on their bikes and peeled out of the quarry. Dylan made it out first.

Levi spied Sweeney at the edge of the group of riders, heading for his car. The quarry cleared out fast, except for the dead or wounded left behind. And Levi still hadn't found Dallas. He left his hiding place and ran for Sweeney's car, but Sweeney beat him to it, jumped in and drove toward the entrance of the quarry.

Levi couldn't let him get away. Dallas might be in that vehicle. Sweeney wouldn't let her go now. He'd kill her first.

DALLAS CAME TO in the dark, a cardboard box digging into her back and her head splitting. For a moment, she couldn't remember where she was, only that it was dark and she was in a cramped space.

Then she remembered she had been looking down into a trunk at what she assumed was the stolen meth. Sweeney must have pushed her in. She felt around, looking for some kind of latch that would open the trunk and allow her to escape. When she didn't find one, she tried kicking at the back of the seat. No matter how hard she kicked, the seat refused to budge.

The car engine started and the vehicle rolled across bumpy ground. "Let me out of here," Dallas called out.

The vehicle didn't slow or stop.

"Let me out or I'll shoot!" she yelled.

"Shut up!" a male voice barked, and the vehicle picked up speed, hitting every bump hard.

It was Sweeney.

Dallas patted her sides and found her weapon where she'd left it, in the holster under her arm. She pulled it out and aimed at what she hoped was the driver and pulled the trigger.

The vehicle swerved to one side. She fired again, and the vehicle swerved in the other direction. She kept firing, praying she'd hit the bastard.

One of her bullets must have done the job. The car suddenly sped up and then hit something hard and rolled, throwing her around like a rag in a washing machine, jarring her head all over again. The vehicle landed on its wheels and bounced before coming to a full stop.

As she lay in the dark trunk, her head spinning, Dallas fought to keep her mind clear. She tried again to kick down the back of the seat, but to no avail.

She finally found the latch that should have opened the trunk. Because the vehicle had rolled, the trunk latch was jammed.

Screaming and pounding against the metal trunk lid only made her head hurt worse. She assumed that since the car had stopped and the engine had died that she must have hit her mark and Sweeney must be dead, or so badly injured that he couldn't do anything to hurt her again.

When no one came to pull her out of the trunk, she wondered if Sweeney had taken her out onto a deserted road somewhere and that there was nobody around who could hear her screams. She didn't stop screaming until her voice grew hoarse and her hands were bruised from banging against the metal.

"Someone, please," she said, "get me out of here." Her head hurt so bad that tears sprang to her eyes as she banged and kicked at the trunk lid. "Someone, anyone, get me out of here." She wondered where Levi was. He was probably still back at Sweeney's Bar, with no way to find her since she had the keys to her truck in her pocket. Just when her voice was reduced to a croaking whisper, she heard voices.

"Dallas!" a familiar voice called out.

"Levi? Levi, is that you?" she called out. "I'm in here!" Dallas beat against the trunk lid again, yelling, even though her voice was more of a croak.

"Dallas." Levi's voice called out much closer this time. "Dallas, where are you?"

"I'm in here," Dallas croaked. "In the trunk of Sweeney's car."

"Hang in there, babe. I'll get you out," Levi called.

"Oh, thank God," she said and lay still, preserving what little strength she had left.

Several long minutes later, the trunk lid was pried open, and Levi stood looking down at her, a crowbar in his hand. His face bathed in moonlight was the most beautiful thing Dallas had ever seen. She reached up her arms.

Levi bent, scooped her out of the trunk and held her against him. "Oh, babe, you had me so worried."

"You were worried?" She laughed and winced. "You weren't the one stuck in the back of a trunk."

"Are you okay?" he asked.

She wrinkled her brow. "Other than a splitting headache, I think I'm gonna live."

"What happened?"

"I was searching Sweeney's trunk. By the way, I found the meth there. Anyway, I was hit from behind with something hard." She reached behind her head and touched it gingerly, wincing. When she brought her hand away, there was blood on it.

Levi frowned. "We need to get you to a hospital."

Dallas wasn't going to argue. "Yeah, maybe we should." She looked toward the front of the car. "What about Sweeney?"

Trace Travis appeared beside Levi, his gun drawn. "I checked him. He's got a pulse, but he's out cold. We need to get an ambulance out here."

"Make it two," Levi added.

"On it," the sheriff responded into his headset. "They're already on their way out."

Within the next five minutes, an ambulance

arrived, with another one right behind it. Levi directed the EMTs to check over Dallas first. The second ambulance's EMTs worked on Sweeney to get him out of the vehicle and onto a stretcher. He was alive but pretty banged up from the wreck and bullet wounds where Dallas's aim had hit her blind mark.

The EMTs loaded Dallas onto a stretcher and into the back of an ambulance. Levi insisted on riding with her, flashing his deputy's badge to get them to let him on board. He held Dallas's hand all the way back to Whiskey Gulch, where they pulled up to the emergency room entrance at the hospital.

Dallas lay with an arm over her eyes. "Did you tell the sheriff I found the meth?" she asked.

"No, but I will now. Where did you find it?"

"It was in the trunk, in a gym bag."

Levi sent a text to the sheriff indicating where the meth could be found.

The sheriff responded, Already found it, bagged it, and transported it back to the station.

Good deal, Levi replied. I'll let Deputy Jones know.

How is she doing?

Suffered a head injury, we'll know more when the doctor has seen her

Take care of her. It's hard to find good help

Will do

When they arrived at the hospital, Dallas was rushed into an exam room, and from there, she was sent off to have a CAT scan.

Levi followed, standing outside the room where they were conducting the scan. When they rolled her back into the examination room in the ER, he parked himself by her bedside.

When the doc came in, Levi pounced. "Well, how is she?"

"She's got quite a goose egg on the back of her head. Fortunately, we didn't see any bleeding on the brain, but we'd like to keep her overnight for observation. We'll move her to a different room."

"I'm going with her," Levi said.

The doctor nodded. "Are you her fiancé or spouse?"

"I could be," he said. "Once we get to know each other a little better."

"I'm not supposed to let anybody but family members be with her," the doctor said.

Levi raked a hand through his hair. They'd all been through hell in that quarry. He didn't need to be stonewalled by a doctor now. He pulled his deputy's star out of his pocket and waved it in front of the doctor. "I'm a deputy sheriff," he said. "This woman is my witness. I'll be with her at all times."

The doctor raised his hands. "All right, then."

A nurse showed up with a gurney, and they transferred Dallas onto it. She winced with every jolt to her head. The nurse wheeled her to the elevator and up to a different floor, where she was then taken into another room. The nurse on that floor took her vitals and recorded them on a computer. When she was satisfied everything was all right, she left the room, dimming the lights as she walked out.

Levi pulled a chair close to the bed and took Dallas's hand in his. He held it late into the night and into the early hours of the morning. Finally, he laid down his head on the bed beside her and slept. He wouldn't leave her side until he knew for sure that she was going to be all right. He wanted her to be all right so that he could explore these feelings he had for her. There was no way she was just a rebound. Everything he felt for Dallas was new, refreshing, and filled him with hope for the future.

In the wee hours of the morning, she stirred. Levi was instantly awake and leaned over her. "Are you okay? Can I get you something to drink?"

She smiled. "I've got a bit of a headache."

"I'll call the nurse," he said.

She tightened the grip on his hands. "No need. I'm sure it will go away soon. Tell me what happened in the quarry."

"I'll tell you all about it later. Right now, you need to rest."

She nodded, too tired to argue with him. "Okay," she said, "on one condition."

He chuckled. "And what's that?"

"You sleep with me," she said.

"I don't know how the nurses will feel about that, but okay." He lowered the side rail, scooted her over on the bed and then climbed in beside her.

She turned on her side to allow him more room, and they wrapped their arms around each other. "Mmm," she said, "that's better."

He kissed the tip of her nose and brushed his lips across hers in a very light kiss.

"You call that a kiss?" she said.

He laughed. "Sleep," he said.

She didn't argue but nestled up against him and was soon asleep.

Levi held her in his arms, loving the feel of her soft body against his and grateful he'd found her alive.

Chapter Fifteen

"I've got the steaks," Rosalynn called out. She carried a tray full of thick beef steaks out on the porch. "How are those baked potatoes coming?"

Trace glanced over his shoulder from his position at the massive grill they'd had specially made for just such occasions on the Whiskey Gulch Ranch. "They should be done about the time the steaks are."

"Here—" Levi leaped up from the porch swing where he'd been sitting with Dallas and took the heavy tray from Rosalynn "—let me." He carried the tray down the steps to Trace and set it on a table beside the grill.

"Anyone hear from Becker?" Irish asked. "Wasn't he supposed to be here today?"

Trace glanced at his watch. "He called this morning and said he'd be here about now."

"I hope he hasn't had any difficulties finding us," Rosalynn said.

"I'm sure his GPS will get him here," Lily said. "Do you have an assignment for him yet?"

Trace shook his head. "I have a couple of clients who are interested, but they haven't committed yet. Once they do, we'll have enough work to keep us busy for a while."

"I take it word is getting out about our services," Matt commented. "Won't be long before we need more help."

"Got that covered as well," Trace said with a smile. "Not only are clients finding us, but guys coming off active duty have started calling, looking for work."

"That's good. I hope more of our old team members find their way to Whiskey Gulch Ranch," Levi said. "It will be nice to eventually have us all back together."

Sheriff Greer arrived with his wife, Beverly, and they settled into a couple of the many rocking chairs lined up on the porch.

"Any news from Sweeney?" Dallas asked.

Levi held his breath, waiting for the sheriff's answer.

The sheriff nodded. "From his account, Sweeney didn't steal the meth. Johnny did, and gave it to him to distribute for a cut in the profits. He swears he never knew where their lab was. Johnny and Jimmy stole the stash."

"Then who killed Harold Sims?" Levi asked as he helped Trace load the steaks onto the grill.

"Johnny and Jimmy told Sweeney they did when Sims stumbled onto their production lab. They told Sweeney that they would do the same to him if he breathed a word to anyone about where he got the stuff."

"Why was Sweeney at the quarry if it was just a meeting of the Snakes?" Trace asked.

The sheriff's mouth twisted. "Sweeney had gone to the quarry to return the stash after he'd heard Johnny had threatened to kill Sean and Evan if they didn't kill him. He was going to out Johnny and return the stolen meth in exchange for his life."

"Then why did he take Dallas?"

"She was in the wrong place at the wrong time," the sheriff said. "And she's lucky the Snakes started shooting each other. It didn't give Sweeney time to hand over the meth and Dallas for disposal."

"Sweeney owned up to that?" Matt asked.

The sheriff nodded. "He swore he wanted nothing to do with killing anyone. That was all on Jimmy and Johnny Marks. And get this…" The sheriff grinned. "Someone placed a call to Judd Marks, letting him know about his brothers' deaths and how low the motorcycle club he'd started had come."

"And?" Trace called out from the grill.

"And he and his wife and children are moving back to Whiskey Gulch to straighten them out. He refused to have his hometown become a battleground."

Dallas clapped her hands. "So, Dylan and Jess won't have to leave?"

The sheriff frowned. "Why would they leave?"

Dallas grinned. "No reason…now. And for anyone who wants to help, I've set up a fund for the couple to help them get established in a house big enough for them and the baby, as well as to help them purchase a car to get the three of them around."

"I'll match any contributions to your fund," Trace said.

Rosalynn smiled at her son. "Your father would have been proud of you. He helped so many in our little community."

Once Trace had all the steaks on the grill, Levi rejoined Dallas on the porch swing. He leaned close and whispered in her ear. "I have something important to ask you."

Dallas shot a startled look in his direction. "Here? Now?"

He nodded. "Will you…?"

She held her breath and reached for his hand. "Will I what?"

"Will you go out with me on an honest-to-goodness date?" He squeezed her hand. "I feel like we have so much in common."

"But we barely know each other," she said, her heart singing.

"True. And I want to remedy that." He brought her hand to his lips. "So, will you?"

She smiled and nodded. "Yes. I'd love to go out with you."

"Do you think we stand a chance as a couple?" he asked. "Please say yes."

She nodded, her eyes filling with joyous tears. "Yes. I think we stand a very good chance."

"Why do you think that?" he whispered into her ear.

She laughed. "Because we have so much in common."

"Like?"

"We like each other," she said. "A lot. At least on my part."

He nodded. "I'd go so far as to say I love you."

Her eyes widened. "So soon?"

He slipped his arm around her shoulders and drew her close. "Sweetheart, life's short. You have to grab for all the happiness you can, while you can. I'm grabbing mine. I hope you'll grab yours, too." He pressed a kiss to her lips. "And I hope I'm the one who makes you happy."

Dallas smiled and cupped Levi's cheek. "You

do. And I'm grabbing." Then she kissed him long and hard.

Someone cleared his throat nearby.

Dallas broke away from Levi, her cheeks heating.

"Are we interrupting something?" Irish asked.

"No," Levi said. "Not at all. We're just kissing. Nothing to see here." He winked.

"It seems our guy Levi now knows the secret we've all discovered since coming to work for the Outriders," Irish noted.

"And what's that?" Dallas asked.

"There is life after the military," Trace said. "Congratulations on making that discovery for yourselves."

"But we wouldn't be the people we are today had we not joined in the first place," Matt said.

All the men nodded their heads as one.

"I wouldn't trade my experience in the army for anything," Trace said. "It makes me even more grateful for what I have today."

Lily left the porch and joined Trace at the grill.

He slipped his arm around her waist and pulled her close for a kiss.

Irish wrapped his arm around Tessa's shoulders. "Coming to work for the Outriders led me to you. And you're the best thing that's ever happened to me."

She smiled into his eyes and brought his head down so she could kiss him.

Aubrey stepped into the circle of Matt's arms. "Aren't you going to tell me I'm the best thing that's ever happened to you?"

"You already know it," he said and pulled her close to his side.

"I think we started something," Levi whispered into Dallas's ear.

"Good." She laughed and threw her arms around his neck. "Now, let's finish it."

Her heart soared, her happiness unequaled. All because of this man, a former Delta Force operative. She was truly blessed to love again.

* * * * *

Get 4 FREE REWARDS!

We'll send you 2 FREE Books _plus_ 2 FREE Mystery Gifts.

FREE Value Over **$20**

Both the **Harlequin Intrigue®** and **Harlequin® Romantic Suspense** series feature compelling novels filled with heart-racing action-packed romance that will keep you on the edge of your seat.

YES! Please send me 2 FREE novels from the Harlequin Intrigue or Harlequin Romantic Suspense series and my 2 FREE gifts (gifts are worth about $10 retail). After receiving them, if I don't wish to receive any more books, I can return the shipping statement marked "cancel." If I don't cancel, I will receive 6 brand-new Harlequin Intrigue Larger-Print books every month and be billed just $5.99 each in the U.S. or $6.49 each in Canada, a savings of at least 14% off the cover price or 4 brand-new Harlequin Romantic Suspense books every month and be billed just $4.99 each in the U.S. or $5.74 each in Canada, a savings of at least 13% off the cover price. It's quite a bargain! Shipping and handling is just 50¢ per book in the U.S. and $1.25 per book in Canada.* I understand that accepting the 2 free books and gifts places me under no obligation to buy anything. I can always return a shipment and cancel at any time. The free books and gifts are mine to keep no matter what I decide.

Choose one: ☐ **Harlequin Intrigue Larger-Print** (199/399 HDN GNXC) ☐ **Harlequin Romantic Suspense** (240/340 HDN GNMZ)

Name (please print)

Address Apt. #

City State/Province Zip/Postal Code

Email: Please check this box ☐ if you would like to receive newsletters and promotional emails from Harlequin Enterprises ULC and its affiliates. You can unsubscribe anytime.

Mail to the **Harlequin Reader Service:**
IN U.S.A.: P.O. Box 1341, Buffalo, NY 14240-8531
IN CANADA: P.O. Box 603, Fort Erie, Ontario L2A 5X3

Want to try 2 free books from another series! Call 1-800-873-8635 or visit www.ReaderService.com.

*Terms and prices subject to change without notice. Prices do not include sales taxes, which will be charged (if applicable) based on your state or country of residence. Canadian residents will be charged applicable taxes. Offer not valid in Quebec. This offer is limited to one order per household. Books received may not be as shown. Not valid for current subscribers to the Harlequin Intrigue or Harlequin Romantic Suspense series. All orders subject to approval. Credit or debit balances in a customer's account(s) may be offset by any other outstanding balance owed by or to the customer. Please allow 4 to 6 weeks for delivery. Offer available while quantities last.

Your Privacy—Your information is being collected by Harlequin Enterprises ULC, operating as Harlequin Reader Service. For a complete summary of the information we collect, how we use this information and to whom it is disclosed, please visit our privacy notice located at corporate.harlequin.com/privacy-notice. From time to time we may also exchange your personal information with reputable third parties. If you wish to opt out of this sharing of your personal information, please visit readerservice.com/consumerschoice or call 1-800-873-8635. **Notice to California Residents**—Under California law, you have specific rights to control and access your data. For more information on these rights and how to exercise them, visit corporate.harlequin.com/california-privacy.

HIHRS22